A Vi  *ian Hills* . . .

Tina Marini: The famous composer's daughter and heir, she killed her husband in self-defense. Now she fears for her own life . . .

Carlo Renzi: Tina's cousin-in-law and scion of an ancient family, he knows that Tina's death would restore Renzi lands into family hands . . .

Luisa Valle: Tina's husband's furiously grieving mistress had the oldest motive of all—vengeance . . .

Susie Brecht: Tina's old school chum knew too well the power of her friend's beauty—well enough to hold a terminal grudge . . .

Emilia Marini and Edmund Traherne: Tina's quite unmaternal and high-living mother and her lover were fast running out of money—and Tina's will promised more . . .

Geraldine Foster: The late composer's last mistress was possessed by violent rages—but could she coolly calculate murder?

LAMENT FOR CHRISTABEL

Books by Audrey Peterson

Lament for Christabel
Elegy in a Country Graveyard
Deadly Rehearsal
Murder in Burgundy
Death in Wessex
The Nocturne Murder

Published by POCKET BOOKS

Most Pocket Books are available at special quantity discounts for bulk purchases for sales promotions, premiums or fund raising. Special books or book excerpts can also be created to fit specific needs.

For details write the office of the Vice President of Special Markets, Pocket Books, 1230 Avenue of the Americas, New York, New York 10020.

LAMENT FOR CHRISTABEL

Audrey Peterson

POCKET BOOKS

New York   London   Toronto   Sydney   Tokyo   Singapore

This book is a work of fiction. Names, characters, places and incidents are either the product of the author's imagination or are used fictitiously. Any resemblance to actual events or locales or persons, living or dead, is entirely coincidental.

An *Original* Publication of POCKET BOOKS

 POCKET BOOKS, a division of Simon & Schuster Inc.
1230 Avenue of the Americas, New York, NY 10020

ISBN: 0-671-72969-1

First Pocket Books printing August 1991

10 9 8 7 6 5 4 3 2 1

POCKET and colophon are registered trademarks of
Simon & Schuster Inc.

Printed in the U.S.A.

For Laura, again

In grateful acknowledgment to the estate of the late Reginald Griffiths of Cumbria, U.K., for the use of his delightful song setting of Coleridge's "Answer to a Child's Question."

LAMENT FOR CHRISTABEL

• 1 •

STRUGGLING THROUGH THE TRAFFIC ACROSS THE RIVER Arno, Andrew Quentin found the road to the Piazzale Michelangelo, following its twisting uphill course. There, through the screening trees, each bend gave a tantalizing glimpse of the city of Florence, farther and farther below. Beyond the Piazzale, past the church of San Miniato, with its formidable tiers of steps, Andrew came at last to the narrow street, hemmed by protective walls, which led in turn to the Via Fiore.

Pretty lucky, he thought, to be invited to stay at Casa Marini. When he first started work on a biography of the composer Piero Marini, he had applied to the widow for access to whatever materials she might have and had been turned down flat. Then, less than a month ago, he had a letter from the daughter, Cristina Renzi, reversing her mother's decision and offering him access to the papers at Casa Marini, even suggesting he might stay there for a month or so, in the annex that contained her father's workroom.

After finishing the summer session, he had lost no time winding things up at the university. His research leave would give him precious time to get on with the project.

At Via Fiore, number seven, Andrew found the gate open and bumped along the gravel drive, stopping a discreet distance from the door. Later, no doubt, he would be told where to put his car.

His ring at the door of the imposing villa produced only an eerie silence. He checked his watch. Eleven o'clock sharp, she had written.

He rang again and waited. Now he heard the soft slap of footsteps, and at last the door was opened by a stout, gray-haired woman who looked at him without speaking.

Andrew cleared his throat. "Signora Renzi?"

The woman's beady eyes scanned him stolidly. *"Il professore americano?"*

"Si."

With a gesture for Andrew to come in and follow her, the woman pointed to a door on the far side of the room, saying in heavily accented English, "On the terrace. Please to wait."

Murmuring *"Grazie,"* Andrew stepped through the doorway and along a short path to a stone bench. From there he caught a Promethean view of the red-tiled roofs of the city below, dominated by the dome of the cathedral and the tower of the Palazzo Vecchio, with the river gleaming green in the hot September sun.

Riveted by the sight, Andrew scarcely noticed that a woman was standing below him, at the bottom of the garden, which dropped steeply in a series of terraces, each level presenting a formal pattern of cypress trees and shrubbery surrounding elegant stone statues. The garden was bounded by a wall, beyond which a grove of olive trees dipped out of sight below.

Then he saw her. The woman lifted her head, looking up toward the house but giving no sign that she saw him. She brought her hands together and

2

stood, like a praying saint, silent and absorbed, gazing into the sun-drenched garden.

Now Andrew heard an angry voice and saw a man emerge from the shrubbery at the bottom of the garden and walk toward the woman. Without hearing the words, Andrew saw them arguing furiously. Starting to turn away in embarrassment, he heard the man snarl and saw him grab the woman by the arm. As she struggled to get free, the man pulled a knife and brought it down toward her. She twisted away, at the same time jabbing her knee into the man's groin.

The man doubled over, dropping the knife. In a flash the woman picked it up and, with a shout of fury, slashed at the man's chest. He struck her brutally across the face, reaching for the knife with his other hand, then suddenly bent over. As Andrew leaped down the steps, the man hobbled toward the wall, where he found a footing and hoisted himself over the top, dropping down out of sight among the olive trees.

Andrew reached the woman as she collapsed with her back against the wall, head bowed, a curtain of glossy black hair shielding her face. The woman moaned, and Andrew saw that blood was pouring from her left arm.

"Ah, signora!" He pulled a not altogether clean handkerchief from his pants pocket and began to tie it over the knife wound on her bare arm, above the elbow.

His textbook Italian not having provided him with appropriate phrases for this kind of emergency, he tried, *"Fa male?"*

Now the sweep of dark hair fell back as she raised her head. Her dark eyes glazed with shock, her delicate mouth trembling, the woman whispered, "You must be Andrew Quentin."

"Yes—"

"I'm Tina Renzi."

Of course—this was Cristina, the daughter.

Andrew looked toward the place where the man had gone over the wall. "Shall I call the police?"

"No, no!"

"He's someone you know?"

"Yes." Bitterly, "He's my husband!"

"Look, you must have a doctor. Can you walk?"

"I don't know. I'll try."

With both his arms around her, Andrew held her against his body. Together, they moved slowly up through the garden to the house, blood splotching his shirt and trousers and streaking her blouse and skirt with shafts of red.

The servant who had opened the door to him appeared, and Tina said in Italian, "Anna, tell Luigi to call the doctor. And bring some towels!"

Stolidly, Anna turned and walked away, while Tina sank into a deep chair, her breathing shallow.

Andrew held tightly to the blood-soaked handkerchief until Anna returned with clean towels, one of which she silently wrapped around her mistress's arm.

Then, loud exclamations in Italian heralded the arrival of Luigi, evidently Anna's husband. The old man's face was a solid mass of lines, like a piece of paper that had been crumpled and spread out again. The lines worked up and down in agitation as he learned from Tina what had happened and assured her the doctor was on his way. His arms gesticulating, his voice hoarse, Luigi spouted what Andrew took to be some pretty unflattering epithets of Signor Renzi, Tina's husband.

At last Tina said, "That's enough, Luigi. This is Professor Andrew Quentin. Will you please show him to his rooms?"

Andrew saw Tina's eyes close, and knowing she would rest better without a stranger present, he followed Luigi to his quarters.

Now he saw that in addition to a well-appointed bedroom and bath, the annex held the spacious room where, over the years, the composer had created many of his best-known works. Somehow, Andrew had pictured the workroom as a barren place with a piano and perhaps a few chairs. What he found was a room of faded but still impressive elegance. There were massive pieces of darkly-carved furniture, oriental carpets, thick velvet draperies, walls covered with paintings, and a magnificent piano in one corner, where tall windows shed light onto the music rack.

An hour later Andrew had unpacked and was sorting out his belongings when Luigi came to take away his bloodstained clothing and summon him to an arbor on the upper terrace, where Tina Renzi lay on a lounge chair, her bandaged arm in a sling.

Taking the chair she indicated, Andrew watched her push back the sweep of black hair from her forehead with her free hand, his senses confirming what his first sight of her had told him—that this woman was incredibly lovely. Dark, expressive eyes, exquisite features, and a body to match. The powerful charge of attraction shook him, making his mouth dry as he asked how she was feeling.

He saw her make an effort to smile. "Not bad. The doctor anesthetized the arm and took some stitches."

Initially, Andrew had offered to drive her to the hospital, only to be met with vigorous opposition, and now Tina explained. "It's a family affair, you understand. Our *dottore* will be discreet. At the hospital a knife wound would be reported to the police. Even a member of the Renzi family couldn't prevent that, and then the newspapers . . . You see?"

Leaning back in his chair, Andrew nodded. "But, Mrs. Renzi—"

Tina smiled again, but her dark eyes regarded him gravely. "Call me Tina, please, if I may call you Andrew?"

"But of course—Tina. The point is, your husband tried to kill you. Will he try it again?"

With a shrug, "How do I know?"

"Has this happened before?"

"He's made threats, yes, and struck me several times. That's why we live apart. But this"—looking at her bandaged arm—"no, this is the first time."

She looked up as the old servant appeared with a tray, which he put down on the table between them. "Thank you, Luigi."

The old man looked at his mistress dolefully and shuffled away.

"Poor Luigi! He's always been my champion since I was a little girl."

Andrew looked down at the crystal pitcher and two glasses on the tray. "Shall I?"

"Please."

The purplish wine had a fresh taste, different from vintage bottles but delicious in its own way.

"Local?" he asked.

"Yes. Nice, isn't it?"

Andrew brushed away the flies attracted to the wine by the midday heat. "Do you mind if I take off my coat?"

Tina laughed. "Of course not! You're awfully formal for an American, Andrew."

"Believe me I'm not! Remember, I expected to meet an imposing Italian signora, not . . ."

"Not what?"

Feeling like an idiot, Andrew found himself saying, "Well, not someone young and beautiful!"

"Thanks for the compliment. But I'm no child, you know. My father was sixty-one when I was born. That makes me thirty. Daughters of famous men can't conceal their age."

Andrew smiled. "I believe your mother is Italian, but you sound quite American."

"Well, my father grew up in New York City, as you probably know, and we always spoke a mixture of English and Italian. Then I was sent to school in the States when I was ten. Soon after, my father died."

"I see. I'd have thought your mother would want to keep you with her for a time."

"Mamma? Not very likely. She had other fish to fry, if you know what I mean. I'd have been sent away sooner, only Babbo wouldn't hear of it."

"Your father?"

"Yes. Italian for Daddy."

"You were fond of him?"

"I loved him." Tina stared into her wineglass, then drank it off and held it out to Andrew.

Refilling their glasses, Andrew said, "It's very good of you to let me stay here at Casa Marini. More than I expected. Your mother refused to give me any help."

"I know. But when Mamma had a stroke and went into the sanitarium, I simply moved in here. I had to get away from Mario—as you can see from what happened today."

"Yes."

"No one has used the annex for years, so I thought you might as well stay here. A lot of Babbo's papers and things are stored away in there. Mamma would never let anyone have access to them when she lived here, although technically they belong to me. Babbo left his papers and royalties to me in his will, but it just wasn't worth hassling with her."

"But won't she object to my being here? You know she refused me an interview last year . . ."

"She's pretty much an invalid now. I don't think she cares anymore."

"Is she living near here?"

"Oh, no. She was in England with Edmund when it happened."

"Edmund?"

"Her companion. They've been together for more than twenty years."

Andrew blinked. "But your father died . . . ?"

Tina's mouth twisted in a bitter smile. "Yes, twenty years ago. Mamma didn't wait around for his demise. Of course, to be fair, Babbo had his own consolations."

"So I have gathered from his previous biographers."

"Yes. It's called marriage Italian style. People don't divorce, they make other arrangements instead. It's the same in most countries where the Church still has influence."

A companionable silence fell between them, Andrew wondering if Tina and her husband would now follow the custom and make their own "arrangements."

At last Andrew said, "Are you in much pain?"

"No, not really. The doctor gave me some tablets, and the wine helps."

"Even so, I think I should go off to a hotel for a few days until you've recovered. Then you can decide if you still want me here."

"Don't be silly. You'll be out in the annex and no trouble at all. Anna and Luigi haven't enough to do as

8

it is, and Anna loves to have people to cook for. She prides herself on her cuisine, so be sure to make a fuss. She'll only glare at you, but she'll be pleased just the same."

As if to prove her point, Luigi arrived with a tray of food for both of them, saying, "You must eat, signora." Andrew had his first sample of Anna's talent, a simple tortellini, but indefinably delicious.

When Luigi had taken away their plates, Tina went upstairs to rest. Andrew, having sent his compliments to the cook, returned to his rooms, intending to finish sorting out his books and notes. Instead, he found himself standing in a daze in the darkened bedroom whose shutters had been closed to keep out the sun, haunted by Tina Renzi's face, feeling again the pressure of her breasts against his body as they struggled up the terrace steps.

With a shrug, he decided there was plenty of time to settle in later, and stretched out on the canopied bed.

Through the haze of too much wine, he drifted into a stuporous drowse, the image of Tina Renzi blurring with visions of his young wife, killed by a teenage driver a few short years ago, pain and desire mingling until at last his eyes closed in sleep.

Some hours later, bathed and in fresh slacks and a cotton shirt, Andrew opened the shutters of his bedroom to a breeze which, while not really cool, gave a pleasant stir to the stifling air.

Hearing a tap on the workroom door, he found Tina Renzi, radiant and smiling, in a green silk dress with a floral scarf as a sling for her injured arm, her dark hair caught in a wide band at the nape of her neck. Diamonds gleamed and swung from her ears.

Feeling more like a teenage Romeo than a man in his thirties, Andrew said, "You look dazzling!"

"Thank you! Are you finding everything you need? Luigi showed you where to ring?"

"Yes, thanks. Everything's marvelous. And your arm?"

"Oh, I'm still taking the pills, but I had promised to go to dinner with friends. No use sitting around feeling sorry for myself!"

And with a "See you tomorrow!" Tina was gone.

◆ 2 ◆

THAT EVENING, ANDREW BEGAN TO EXPLORE THE HALF-dozen cabinets in Marini's workroom, each one bursting with papers and music scores, a few items neatly stacked, but most in a chaos of disorder. Not ordinarily given to regarding famous men with undue reverence, Andrew nevertheless felt a quickening pulse as he saw that he had before him a scholar's dream of buried treasure, and he could scarcely believe his luck in being the first to have access to it.

Marini's previous biographers had had to work without the cooperation of the family, and Andrew had assumed he would suffer the same fate when he got the letter from Tina's mother. In a nearly illegible hand, she had written, "I have nothing to say about the life of my husband. Others have asked, and my answer is no."

Now Andrew lifted a stack of material from the first cabinet and laid it on the huge library table which had served Marini as a desk. Here were pages of manuscript, the notes carelessly jotted on the music staves, comprising early versions of works now familiar to the world, some dating back to the 1920s, when Marini had first left the Italian ghetto in New York City where he grew up and come to live in Italy.

Fascinated, Andrew carefully turned each item, finding a variety of sketches for other works he didn't recognize, some evidently abandoned, others used or modified. Personal items were mixed freely with musical scores. Between two sheets of music was a bill for a case of wine, and later, a receipt for two pairs of handmade shoes, and farther down in the stack a sheet of blue notepaper folded in half. *Carissimo,* it read, *Vengo domani!* Andrew smiled. "Dearest, I'll come tomorrow."

Eventually he tore himself away from Marini's papers and went to bed, visions of Tina Renzi invading his sleep.

The next morning, intrigued as he was by the materials he had discovered, Andrew nevertheless found himself looking up from his notes from time to time, hoping Tina might tap on the door of the workroom.

But when the tap came, it was Luigi, looking distressed. *"Mi scusi, signore.* Please to come."

Alarmed, Andrew tossed his pen on the table and followed Luigi along the passage that connected the annex to the house.

In the salon, Andrew saw a tableau that stopped him in his tracks. Tina sat in a high-backed chair, flanked by two uniformed policemen.

Swiftly, he crossed the room and pressed her hand for a moment. "What is it?"

"It's Mario. He's dead."

"Your husband?"

"Yes. It seems I killed him."

"You?"

"Yes. His body was found this morning down the hill below the wall. Some boys were playing in the undergrowth and found him."

"Do you mean this happened yesterday, when—"

"Yes, it must have been. They tell me he died of a knife wound in the chest. He's been dead since yesterday. He must have died soon after he went over the wall. I *did* strike back at him. I wanted to frighten him away."

"But surely it was in self-defense. He tried to kill you—I saw him!"

"That's what I've told them."

One of the officers handed Andrew a photograph of the corpse, asking in Italian if this was the man he saw.

Nodding to Tina to indicate that he understood, Andrew studied the picture. Dark, wavy hair, stocky build, wearing a red and green checkered shirt. Yes, certainly, this was the man he had seen.

Tina's mouth trembled. "I must go to identify the body. Then they want to question both of us."

Half an hour later Andrew sat in the office of the Questura Polizia, the central police station in Florence, being questioned by a detective officer who spoke some English, while Tina Renzi was interviewed in another room. In the police car that brought them here, Tina had murmured to him, "I still can't believe it. I felt the knife go into his flesh, but I never imagined it went deep enough to harm him!"

"Wouldn't he have fallen if the blow was that serious?"

"No, the officer told me people with stab wounds sometimes walk around, not even realizing they've been hurt. Then later they collapse."

Now, in answer to the detective officer's question,

Andrew said, "I saw Signora Renzi and her husband at the bottom of the garden."

"At what time was this, please?"

"About eleven o'clock in the morning."

"And what took place at that time?"

"They appeared to be angry."

"Could you hear what was said?"

"No, not the words, but it was obvious they were quarreling."

"And then?"

Andrew described in detail what he had seen as he stood by the stone bench on the upper terrace.

"When Signor Renzi first dropped the knife, had the signora been stabbed at that time?"

"Yes, it had cut her left arm, but I didn't know that until afterward. Her right side was turned toward me."

"When Signor Renzi dropped the knife, could the signora not have run off and escaped from him at that time?"

Andrew pondered. "Maybe if she hadn't been injured, she might have got away, but she must have been shocked by the stab wound to her arm. When I reached her moments later, she had almost fainted, and the blood was gushing from the wound. I'm afraid her husband would have caught up with her if she had tried to run, and he might well have killed her."

"Afterward, was the signora afraid that her husband was seriously hurt?"

"No. She had no idea her blow could have been fatal. She thought she had succeeded in scaring him off."

A second officer conferred with the first, listened to Andrew's story again, then asked him to sign a statement.

"It will be translated into English for you, signor."

Explaining that he could read Italian fairly well, just not speak rapidly enough for conversation, Andrew waited and was duly presented with a statement in Italian for his signature.

"The signora's statement is being prepared. Do you wish to leave now?"

"No, thank you, I'll wait for the signora."

When Tina at last emerged, she stood before Andrew, looking up at him, her eyes cloudy with pain. With a trembling hand, she pushed the dark curtain of hair from her forehead. Adjusting the sling on her left arm, she said, "Let's walk, shall we?"

When they reached the street, Tina stood still, frowning. "Something odd. The police told me they found Mario's car on the road below the house. It had been parked there since yesterday."

Andrew said, "He must have come up the hill and over the wall."

"Yes." Then she shrugged. "Let's get something to eat. There's a place I like down this way."

After a short walk, they turned into a street so narrow they had to flatten against the nearest wall as a car came through.

At the restaurant, a pitcher of wine between them, Tina suggested the saltimbocca, which turned out to be excellent.

"Just don't tell Anna," she cautioned. "I always tell her I had a pizza if I eat lunch out. She brooks no competition with food!"

Andrew smiled, and they chatted amiably, skimming over the surface of their lives—her school days in New York City, his in California—and discovered a shared fondness for England, where both had spent a good deal of time.

"Your father had a place in the Lake District, didn't he?" asked Andrew.

"Yes, near Keswick, where the poet Coleridge lived. Babbo loved to go there in the summer and fall. I still have the place—he left it to me. Mamma hated it—it was so isolated and cold most of the year. That's where my father died, you know."

"Yes, I remember."

Tina smiled. "Of course, you've been researching him for ages, haven't you? You probably know more about him than I do."

"One thing I don't know is how he met his death. There seems to be some mystery surrounding the circumstances of his drowning."

"Yes. It was very late at night when he fell into the lake below the house. There was a lot of talk that it might have been suicide, but the coroner's verdict called it accidental death."

"What do you think?"

"Oh, it must have been an accident. Babbo wasn't the type to take his own life. At least, so it seemed to me. I was only ten, but I think I would have known."

"Were you there at the time?"

"Yes. I was sleeping in an upstairs bedroom. Some sound woke me up, and I looked out the window and saw my father sitting on a bench at the end of the dock. Later, I thought I heard something fall into the water. I ran downstairs and through the garden to the edge of the lake. When we found he was missing, we called for help, but it was too late. He couldn't swim, you know."

Andrew paused. "Look, Tina, I'm so sorry. We shouldn't be talking about death. This is hardly the time . . ."

Tina stared down at the tablecloth, then looked up

at Andrew, her eyes shadowed. "It's all right. I brought it up. I suppose one death makes you think of another, doesn't it? The truth is, Andrew, I'm glad Mario's dead."

• 3 •

THROUGH THE REMAINDER OF THEIR LUNCH, ANDREW AND Tina stuck to innocuous topics of food and travel, but as they lingered over their coffee, Tina said, "Andrew, I need to talk about Mario. I want you to understand why I said what I did."

"Of course."

"We were married six years ago. I was twenty-four, Mario was older—thirty-two. His father had died the year before, and he had lost his mother when he was at school. The Renzis are an old Tuscan family, fairly rich, although not so much so as in the past. All the good families are affected by taxation and inflation.

"In the beginning, we were very much in love. Mario sometimes had a vile temper, but after his rages he was so contrite and loving that I forgave him everything. The real trouble began when I was unable to have children. Mario wanted a child desperately, to continue the family name, and I wanted a child because I loved him."

Tina brushed back her hair with an impatient gesture.

"For a long time I had had severe menstrual pain every month, and the doctors diagnosed endometriosis, which makes conception difficult at best. Finally, the condition became so severe they had to do a hysterectomy. While I was ill and recuperating, Mario was wonderful to me, but afterward I think it began to gnaw at him that children were now impossible.

"He began to have affairs with various women, not even trying very hard to conceal them. Of course this is common enough for Italian husbands, but it hurts the wife nevertheless. Then he met Luisa Valle, and I soon sensed that this was not the usual fling, but something serious.

"We quarreled constantly over her. Luisa's husband had died and she was free to marry. She's about my age and already has a child, so I knew this was a big factor for Mario. I offered to give him a divorce, but he just laughed and said Renzis don't divorce. Besides, what good would that do, when the church wouldn't recognize a second marriage while the first wife is still alive?

"A few months ago he began striking me when he was angry, and gradually it came to me that he really wanted me dead."

Andrew looked across the table at Tina's lowered head. On an impulse, he gently lifted the fall of silken hair that covered her brow.

As she looked up, startled, he said simply, "I'm glad, too, that Mario's dead."

When they left the restaurant, they strolled along to the Via Cavour, turning in the direction of the Duomo. As they came to the corner where the forbidding exterior of the Medici-Riccardi Palace loomed, Tina said, "I'd like to go up to the little chapel. Do you want to come?"

"Yes, of course. Only I'm afraid we'll see more police as we go in."

At the entrance to the courtyard of the palace was the office of the Prefettura, where uniformed policemen of the Tuscan district had their headquarters, separate from the Questura Polizia, the local police station where they had been questioned.

Tina grimaced as they passed into the courtyard. "You're right. I've seen enough police for one day!"

Silently they climbed the wide marble staircase to the exquisite little chapel that Cosimo di Medici had had designed for his private use. Between the fluted pilasters, the artist Gozzoli had covered every inch of the walls with his frescoes of fifteenth century Florentine life, mixing religious processions with scenes of secular life, where villas and castles seemed to float in a fantastic landscape of cliffs, woods, and fields.

A family of tourists was leaving the chapel as they came in. Seeing that they were alone, Tina walked quickly to the altar in the raised section of the chapel, kneeling and making the sign of the cross. Andrew could see her lips moving, and he stepped away across the marble floor to study the frescoes on the far wall.

When Tina again stood in front of him, she gently put a hand on his arm, saying, "I'm glad you're here, Andrew."

In the taxi that delivered them back to the house, Tina had been silent and exhausted, saying, "I must rest now, but later on, come and have coffee on the terrace."

Andrew turned left from the main door to the house, following a path to the separate entrance into the L-shaped annex. The large workroom was an extension of the front of the house, while the bath and bedroom wing thrust out onto the terrace at the left side of the property, where a line of cypresses followed the bordering wall to the bottom of the garden.

Expecting to get back to work, Andrew went straight to his desk, only to discover that his mind refused to cooperate. Giving up, he kicked off his shoes, lay on the bed, and fell into a restless sleep. Nightmare visions assailed him, of Tina being assaulted by a man in a red-and-green-checked shirt who disappeared, leaving him to find her body lying on the floor, covered with blood.

When he awoke, groggy and depressed, a tepid bath revived his spirits. Dressed and ready for the promised coffee, he opened the bedroom shutters and heard the sound of voices at the other end of the terrace.

As Andrew approached, he saw Tina reclining on a lounge chair under the arbor, her injured arm propped on a cushion. She was smiling at a young woman in shorts and running shoes whose sandy hair looked as if it had been chopped rather than styled.

Handing Andrew a cup of coffee, Tina said, "Susie, this is Andrew Quentin. My friend, Susan Brecht."

Susie's light blue eyes checked Andrew out. "So you're the professor! I expected a graybeard with rimless spectacles. Are you married?"

Tina stirred. "Susie, really!"

"No harm in asking, is there? The good ones are usually taken. I should know."

"Andrew *was* married—his wife died."

"Oh, I *am* sorry."

Now Andrew looked at Tina in surprise. "How did you know?"

Apologetically, Tina said, "I telephoned your university and spoke to the woman who is chair of your music department. She told me. I couldn't very well ask you to stay at the house without getting a sort of character reference, if you see what I mean?"

"Of course. She did tell me you had talked to her. I just didn't realize—"

"You see, I also needed to know whether you would be coming with a wife and possibly a family in tow!"

"Yes, I understand."

Susie grinned. "So now we have a widow in the house."

Tina gave Andrew a despairing look. "Susie's hopeless. The word 'tact' is unknown in her vocabulary. But I forgive her everything. We were at school together in New York, and I'm afraid I would have left a trail of dead nuns at the Convent of the Sacred Heart if it hadn't been for Susie. She kept me sane."

Susie laughed. "That went both ways, Andrew, let me tell you. Tina's had a rough time lately. She told me what happened yesterday. Thank God you were here. I wouldn't trust the Italian police. They'll always defend men against women. It's a totally macho society."

Andrew looked at Tina. "But if your husband's been violent toward you for some time, wouldn't they believe it was self-defense on your part?"

Tina frowned. "Whenever he struck me, it was naturally when we were alone. I never thought of it that way, but the police might have doubted my word."

Susie snorted. "You told *me* about it often enough. I'd have told them a thing or two. Anyhow, it's a good thing we took that class in how to defend ourselves against attack in the streets of good old New York. When you gave him that knee to the groin, it probably saved your life."

Tina shuddered. "It was so strange. I hadn't thought about the class for years, but when Mario raised that knife, I just reacted without thinking, and it worked! Only I didn't mean to . . ."

"To kill him, you mean." Susie looked at Andrew. "I'd say it was a lucky thing she did, wouldn't you?"

Remembering his confused siesta dream, Andrew

saw again the vision of Tina's body in a pool of blood and was swept with a feeling of desolation so keen it swelled in his throat. Hoarsely, he whispered, "Yes, I think it was."

Tina said, "Thanks, you two. So, Susie, how's Alex?"

Susie shrugged. "What can I say?" Then, to Andrew, "I'm living with this crazy Greek artist at the moment. Or rather, he's living with me, since it's my place."

Tina said, "Susie has an apartment in town by the river. She's an art dealer."

"That sounds impressive, Andrew, but actually I dabble in the art racket on a pretty small scale. I buy stuff here in Italy from contemporary painters like Alex and sell them in England and the States. It gives me a good excuse to keep a place here. By the way, Tina, does Carlo know about Mario?"

"Yes. When the police found our address in Mario's wallet and went to the house, Carlo was there."

To Andrew, Tina said, "Carlo is Mario's cousin."

Susie frowned. "He'll tell Luisa, of course."

"Yes. They'll blame me, I know they will."

"Too bad if they do. At least you're alive!"

Refilling their coffee cups, Susie said to Andrew, "Carlo used to hate Luisa, but lately they've been fairly chummy, heaven knows why."

A silence fell, as a breeze moved the sparse brownish grape leaves that still clung to their vines over the arbor.

Now Luigi's voice was heard from the house, protesting, *"Signora, aspetti, per favore!"*

But it was obvious that the signora, whoever she was, would not wait. Her voice rising, a short, plump woman outran Luigi and rushed toward Tina, her fist clenched. Seeing Andrew and Susie, she stopped a foot from the chaise where Tina lay, screaming out her fury. Andrew had no trouble following the gist of her message. "You killed him! You killed my Mario! You bitch! You made his life a misery!"

Tina simply stared back, her dark eyes stricken. But Susie leaped to her feet, shouting, *"Luisa, basta così!"*

While the battle raged, Andrew looked with surprise at Luisa, wondering how Mario Renzi could have preferred this woman to his wife? While admittedly attractive, Luisa had none of Tina's delicate, haunting beauty.

Abruptly, Luisa's fury sputtered out. Turning, she swept past the hovering Luigi and vanished into the house. A moment later they heard the motor of a car grinding as it sped off.

◆ **4** ◆

BY THE NEXT AFTERNOON, AS ANDREW EXAMINED THE stacks of papers from the shelves in Piero Marini's studio, he was increasingly fascinated by the material he was examining. Even the average music lover would find some interest in early versions of a familiar work, while to the scholar, the fragments and sketches were bits of gold.

By preserving the order in which items had been laid on the shelves, Andrew had thought at first he might establish some chronology, but he soon discovered that chaos was the composer's way of life. A good thing, for had Marini taken the trouble to clear out his cupboards, much of this harvest would have been tossed into the fire. Fortunate, too, that in the years since Marini's death, nothing had been disturbed.

Business letters were usually dated, but the dating of other material depended chiefly on context. Some remained obscure, while others were easily identified. One of these was a letter signed "Emilia," who was to become Tina's mother, writing that she was sure now of her pregnancy and they had better get on with the plans for the wedding.

Emilia, aged twenty-five at the time of their marriage, must still have been living at home in Siena with her parents, for in the letter she complained that her mother wailed at her night and day over her plan to marry a divorced man, and one so many years older than she. "But never mind, my darling. I love you madly"—*Sono innammorata pazza di té*—"Soon I shall tell her I'm expecting your child, and that will keep her quiet!"

In fact, the couple were married in England, where Cristina Emilia was born six months later, in the house in the Lake Country which was Marini's second home.

Carefully sorting the materials in the workroom, Andrew established a tentative organization, making a notecard for each item and using the emptied shelves to house the new groupings. Now, his primary need was to rent a photocopy machine and obtain written permission to copy and use the material.

Mentioning this to Tina when she came to the workroom to invite him to coffee, he asked if she was sure she was willing to give her consent.

"Of course. Just give me the sheet and I'll sign it now." Amused, she added, "You really love all this, don't you?"

Andrew grinned. "How did Balboa feel when he discovered the Pacific? By the way, another great find today. A song setting of a Coleridge poem, only this one was never published."

"Yes, Babbo loved Coleridge and Wordsworth and all the Lake poets. Living in Keswick, we were in the heart of their countryside. What's this one called?"

"'Answer to a Child's Question.'"

"Oh!" Tina's dark eyes looked into Andrew's face. "I remember. It goes like this."

Stepping to the piano, she played and sang the opening bars of the song:

"Babbo wrote it not long before he died. That's probably why it was never published. We were at the house at the lake. He wrote it for me, and he often asked me to sing it when people came."

"Did you like that?"

"I didn't mind singing it for Babbo, but Gerry was living with us by that time, and she always sat there smirking and taking all the credit. After all, it *is* a love song, you know."

"Yes, of course. It ends with 'I love my love and my love loves me.' Rather a mouthful to speak, but in the song it's lovely."

Andrew saw the frown on Tina's face at the recollection of Geraldine Foster, her father's last mistress.

"You didn't like Miss Foster?"

Tina shuddered. "Not much."

At a knock on the door, Luigi came in to announce the arrival of *un signore della polizia.*

Telling Luigi to show the gentleman from the police to the terrace, Tina raised an eyebrow. "Maybe Susie's right and they don't believe me."

"Shall I stay here?"

"No, please come!"

On the terrace the officer, not in uniform, introduced himself, explaining that as Vice Questore he was now assigned to the Renzi case and must ask Signora Renzi to describe again the circumstances of her husband's death.

Andrew, finding that he could follow the Italian quite well when the context was predictable, listened as Tina again recounted what had happened on the day of Mario's death. Then, with her help, he described what he had seen.

Courteously, the officer asked him to indicate precisely where he was at the time, and Andrew led the way along the short path to the stone bench where he had stood and watched the scene in the garden below.

Now the officer asked them if they would kindly reenact what had occurred, with Andrew taking the role of Mario.

With the idiotic feeling that he was a student in a drama class, Andrew followed Tina to the bottom of the garden, going through the motions of the scene he had witnessed. When he raised his arm, gripping the imaginary knife and stabbing downward toward Tina, he saw the horror in her eyes as she relived that daunting moment.

They finished the reenactment in a kind of bizarre slow motion, with Andrew limping toward the wall, looking for the foothold Mario had used to make his leap over the top.

Running lightly down the steps to join them, the officer added to the grotesquerie by exclaiming "Bravo!" as if, thought Andrew bitterly, they were on an opera stage.

"Now, signora, precisely where did your husband ascend the wall?"

"Just here." Tina pointed to the hollow in the plaster.

"But how was he able to find this spot?"

"Oh, I had told Mario how, as children, my friends and I used to slip over the wall to play in the olive grove. There is a little clearing down the hill which makes a wonderful hideaway. Actually, we both climbed over one day and I showed him the place."

"I see. That is, in fact, where your husband's body was found. And one more question, if you please. Why did your husband climb over the wall on this occasion, instead of returning in the normal way through the house?"

Tina frowned. "I've wondered a lot about that. At first I thought it was because he was as frightened of me when I stabbed at him as I had been of him. But when I realized he left his car down there, I changed my mind. Where was it exactly?"

With one accord they turned to look over the wall, Andrew tall enough to see over the top, the officer rising on his toes, Tina putting a foot into the aperture and holding to the top with her good right arm.

Andrew saw how sharply the hill dropped, the dusty gray-green of the olive trees making a canopy over the thickets of undergrowth. Below, through the trees and the roofs of houses, snippets of a winding road were visible.

"The car of Signor Marini was found directly below."

"I see. Thank you."

As they walked slowly back toward the house, the officer waited until they reached the upper terrace before speaking. "And what do you believe now, signora, was the reason for your husband's action?"

Tina faced the officer. "I believe he planned it all. As you know, I had come to live here in my mother's house because of my husband's violence toward me. When Mario came that morning, he said, 'Let's talk in the garden,' and immediately began a violent argument about money. I insisted that if I must live on my own, I should have an adequate allowance, and he wanted to give me a mere pittance. We were both very angry. But why, I ask you, should he have a knife with him?"

"He was not in the habit of carrying one?"

"No. I believe he *planned* to kill me. He could escape over the wall to his car below and leave the police to think I had been attacked by a stranger!"

• 5 •

THE DAY AFTER THE VISIT OF THE POLICE OFFICER, ANDREW heard a knock on the door of the studio in the late morning. Calling *"Avanti!"* he looked up to see Tina coming swiftly toward him, smiling. Her arm was still heavily bandaged, but the sling was gone.

Perched on the edge of his worktable, she said, "Andrew, they've closed the case on Mario's death. The officer who was here yesterday rang me up just now to say they were completely satisfied. Then he went on to express his sympathy for my loss in the gushiest terms, as if they had never had any doubt."

"Oh, good news! At least we won't have to do another dramatic scene. Once was enough for me. It made me realize how near to death you were, Tina . . ."

Looking down at him, the cascade of her dark hair almost touching his face, she said gently, "Thank you for caring."

Then, with a quick change of mood, she smiled. "Look, you can take a break, can't you? How about a picnic? I'll have Anna put up a lunch for us."

Half an hour later they set off in Tina's Ferrari.

"I'll drive," she had said, and Andrew laughed. "I won't argue with that. Italian drivers leave me spitless. But your arm?"

"It's much better, really."

As they started off down the hill, Tina asked, "Have you ever been to San Miniato?"

"Once, long ago, but I'd like to go again."

"Good. Then we'll stop on the way."

"Still plenty of tourists, I see," Tina remarked as she parked the car along the road that skirted the second level of steps leading up to the church, "although the biggest crush is over by this time in September."

Slowly they climbed up the wide stone steps, past the enclosed cemetery with its incongruously modern tombstones, to the simplicity of the basilica itself, where the original rough brown stone had been faced with the green and white marble so dear to the hearts of the thirteenth century Florentine artists.

In the dark interior of the church they stood at the back, letting their eyes adjust, their gaze drawn inevitably to the lighted altar and gold-encrusted chapel glowing at the end of the long nave.

"I love this place," Tina said quietly. "I don't know why. Ancient churches are a dime a dozen all over Italy."

Andrew smiled. "And each one is different. No mass production, even in the same time period."

When they had wandered down the right aisle, up the stairs to the gorgeously frescoed sacristy, down into the crypt and back along the far aisle, Andrew found himself staring into an elegantly adorned side chapel, which he remembered vaguely from his first visit to Florence back in his student days.

As Tina moved on, Andrew remained transfixed. On his right, in a recessed niche, was a marble tomb adorned with the usual cherubs and angels, topped by a bas-relief madonna and child, all very ornate. But what gripped his attention was the panel on the opposite wall of the little chapel, an annunciation, where an already pregnant Mary sits with downcast eyes, one hand at her waist, the other raised, accepting the news that she will bear a Christ child. The glowing red of her gown contrasted with the blue robe draped over her knees, while a filmy veil covered her hair and framed a charming face, the exquisite mouth almost but not quite smiling.

Andrew felt Tina's tug at his arm. "Ready? What's so fascinating?"

"It's the madonna. She looks like you!"

Tina bent forward and peered into the dim light of the chapel. "Oh, do you think so? All those Marys look alike to me."

They walked out into the blinding sunlight, where the city lay below in all its spectacular splendor.

Andrew said, "Of course you have something like this view at home, so it must lose its charm for you."

"No, never. There's nothing quite like it anywhere, is there?"

A long drive up through hills toward Fiesole, where the brown autumn drought was relieved by groves of trees and patches of green, brought them at last to a spot on a hillside where Tina stopped the car.

"Here we are. It's over the crest of the hill."

Laden with picnic gear, they trudged up a dry, unpromising path which skirted the top of the hill and went down again sharply into what proved to be a wooded glade complete with a stream, in which a meager trickle had survived the long heat of the summer.

In the welcome shade of the trees, Andrew spread a quilt over the stubby grass and poured the wine while Tina laid out Anna's sandwiches and fruit. With the hunger invariably produced by being in the open air, they ate till only crumbs were left.

Stretched out with her head on a cushion, Tina sighed.

"I'm glad I found this place, Andrew. I never came here with Mario, so it's been a long time since I was here. Susie and I found it one day."

He felt an absurd pleasure in knowing she hadn't come to this place with her husband or, evidently, with another man, although why he felt this was not something he wanted to analyze.

Softly, Tina said, "Tell me about your wife."

Usually reticent on the subject, Andrew found that he wanted to talk about Norma.

"What words can describe her? Adorable. Merry. As in Gershwin's song, embraceable. We were introduced by a mutual friend in the university bookstore and began with a joke."

Andrew paused, smiling, remembering.

Tina waited, then murmured, "A joke?"

"Yes. In her book bag I saw the top of a French textbook and a can of tennis balls. Then I noticed her fingers were stained with paint, so I did a Sherlock and said I could see the lady was an artist who spoke French and was fond of tennis. She said, 'Quite right, Mr. Holmes,' or something like that, and we all laughed.

"We saw each other constantly after that. There were never any doubts—we knew we were in love almost at once. We were both graduate students and didn't have much money, but it never mattered. We lived together for a while, and when I finished my last degree and was hired at the university in Los Angeles, we were married."

"Children?"

Pain crossed Andrew's face. "No. We had just decided to start a family when she was killed. She went out to mail a letter, and a sixteen-year-old boy, out with friends in his father's car, came around a corner at high speed and struck her. She was in a coma for hours—and then she died."

Tina was silent, her dark eyes speaking for her.

Andrew's fist tightened, then relaxed. "I went through a terrible stage of anger—at the boy, at the fates for meting out such a senseless blow. But it was all inside. I went on teaching that term. It was like being split into two separate identities. One went on functioning—lecturing, reading student exams, bringing tapes and records to class, preparing for my seminar—while the other identity stormed and raged and wept. Gradually, the fury seeped away and left me hollowed out, empty."

"Have you any family?"

"Yes. My parents and a married sister live in Los Angeles. They had adored Norma, which meant they were grieving also. Her parents, too, were devastated. They live in the Midwest, and fortunately there is a large family, with many grandchildren, to ease the burden for them. For myself, I learned that nothing actually helps, except time."

"How long has it been since she died?"

"Five years."

"And you were married for how long?"

"Three years and two months."

"Three years." Tina lay back again, looking up at the trees. "If Mario had died when we had been married for three years, I would have felt as you did—anguished, shattered. Then came my surgery and the change in Mario. He began to be so cruel to me, Andrew. I know it sounds appalling, but all the passionate love I had for him curdled like milk in the hot sun. By the end of that year, I hated him."

In the silence, Andrew raised himself on one elbow and looked down at her, where the light through the leaves stippled her face.

Her eyes half closed, Tina went on. "That was three years ago. That's when I really lost Mario. It's as if he died to me then."

"Yes."

Now Tina's eyes scanned his face. She spoke with no trace of coquetry, only concern: "You're a most attractive man, Andrew. Isn't there someone special in your life?"

He smiled. "No, I'm the despair of my friends, I'm

afraid. Of course I've dated. I'm no monk. But if a woman is looking for marriage—and I'm not ready for that—well, you see, it's awkward—"

"But hasn't there been someone you truly fancied, as the English say?"

"I've been attracted, yes, but I suppose you might say the rockets haven't really gone off. And for you, Tina? Surely you were entitled to have some consolation of your own?"

"Yes, I'd say I was. But my situation was different from yours. Mario was not in fact dead, but was playing the Don Juan left and right. I did have an affair, maybe hoping to make him jealous, or just to get even, I don't know. But it's not a great way of life, at least not for me."

Presently, they gathered up the picnic things and rode back down through the hills in companionable silence. For Andrew, their talk had stirred emotions he could no longer deny. Looking at Tina as she drove—her thickly springing hair falling to her shoulders, the delectable curves of her body, her face so like the enchanting painting at San Miniato—he knew without doubt what he had been feeling almost from that first day: that the rockets had gone off for him at last.

But there was no sign they had done so for Tina.

• 6 •

OVER THE NEXT TEN DAYS OR SO, ANDREW FOUND THAT HE and Tina had casually established a daily routine. Some days she sent for him to share luncheon with her in the dining room, where the light from half-closed shutters fell against green walls, making him feel they were marooned in a deep sea cavern. On the other days, Luigi arrived in the workroom at half-past twelve with a tray, the signal that Tina was out that day. In the evenings, Tina either went out or retired early, while Andrew found that the television in his bedroom gave him excellent practice with his Italian.

But whether they met at other times or not, they usually met on the terrace for coffee in the late afternoon, a ritual Andrew looked forward to with pleasure.

Sometime in the second week after his arrival, when the heat had given way to a promise of autumn in the air, Andrew sat on the terrace with his long legs stretched out, looking at Tina as she lay on the chaise.

Ever since the day of their picnic, Tina had been occupied at the house she had shared with her husband, going through his papers and sorting out personal belongings.

Now she said, "The lawyers and the accountants have sent people out to help me, but it's all pretty confusing, and Carlo keeps arguing about everything. The money and the property go partly to Carlo and partly to me. The house is lovely, but I don't want to live there again—too many unhappy associations.

Carlo wants it, as his branch of the family has lost most of their money."

"Can't you sell the house?"

Tina smiled. "Families like the Renzis don't sell their houses. It isn't done! No, I'd like to stay on here, but technically this house belongs to Mamma, coming to me after her death."

"Surely she'll let you stay here?"

"You don't know Mamma. Not only is she physically impaired by her stroke, she's really gone off the rails." Tina tapped her forehead. "When I called to tell her Mario had died, she went into some long story about seeing him in a vision. It was awful. She's always resented me because Babbo made a will leaving me the bulk of the royalties from his works, so her income hasn't been as great as she would like. Edmund has money, but it's never enough for Mamma."

"She and Edmund have never married?"

"No, that would have made it worse, as she would have lost the allowance from my father's estate if she remarried."

"I see."

"Mamma thinks I'm staying here temporarily. If she knows I really want to stay on, she'll insist on coming back just to spite me, even though Edmund prefers to live near London. He has a very pleasant house in Hampstead, and they've always divided their time between the two places. When Mamma comes out of the sanitarium, Edmund wants her to stay near her doctors in England."

As Tina reached for the coffee urn to refill their cups, Luigi appeared to say the signora was wanted on the telephone.

"Don't go away, Andrew. I'll be right back."

But it was fully ten minutes before Tina came back to the arbor.

"Speaking of the devil—that was Edmund! He's an absolute idiot with money. Instead of leaving his capital safely invested, he took out a chunk of it a few years ago and put it into some scheme that was supposed to double in no time at all. Needless to say, he lost it. Now he's done it again. I bailed him out that time, but I vowed I wouldn't do it a second time."

"Will your mother be—well, very short of money?"

"No, of course not. But they spend their money like water, and Mamma wouldn't know how to cut back. The sanitarium is costing them a bundle, but Edmund says that fortunately she'll be home soon. At first he oozed with charm on the phone, but when I told him my own affairs were in a tangle and I couldn't do anything for him, he turned nasty, in that icy way he has."

The next day Andrew, resigned to waiting till their afternoon coffee for a glimpse of Tina, felt a leap of joy when Luigi summoned him to lunch in the dining room.

As he approached, he saw her sitting at the end of the long, dark table, a fragile figure, drooping, fatigued.

"You're looking very tired," he said gently.

Tina looked up as he took his chair across the corner of the table, languidly pushing the black curtain of hair from her forehead. "Yes. I'm sick of all those papers."

In the darkened room the greenish light fell on the row of carved chairs, looming like sentinels under the tarnished chandeliers, and cast jade shadows on Tina's pale skin.

Over lunch they exchanged a few remarks, Tina preoccupied but making an obvious effort to respond.

When the plates had been cleared and they sat with their coffee, Andrew said firmly, "What is it, Tina? Something's bothering you. Tell me."

"I can't." Her eyes again looked into his. "It may be nothing."

"If it concerns you, I want to know. Are you afraid of something?"

She shook her head, eyes glinting with tears. "It's all right. I wanted to tell you but I can't. I must go."

As she stood up, Andrew caught her hand. "Tina, please!"

Hoarsely, she whispered, "It sounds crazy, but I think someone's trying to kill me!"

And then she was gone. He could hear her footsteps going up the stairs to the bedroom wing of the house.

Andrew went out to the terrace early for their afternoon coffee, determined to break through Tina's reserve and find out what was going on. When a quarter of an hour had passed and she hadn't appeared, he went in search of Luigi.

"The signora?" he asked.

"É partita!"

"Gone?"

Luigi looked at him dolefully, explaining that the signora had come downstairs after luncheon, carrying a suitcase, and told Anna she would be away for some time. "If you asked, Signor Quentin, we were to tell you not to worry."

Knowing it was useless, he nevertheless asked, "Do you know where she has gone?"

"No, signor. She would not say."

Thanking Luigi, he declined his offer of coffee and wandered back to the terrace.

"If I asked," he muttered. "She must know I would

37

ask." But after all, what right had he to Tina's confidence? A picnic, a few lunches, coffee on the terrace. She had given no sign that he was more than a pleasant distraction in her life.

Pacing the terrace, with the image of Tina's haggard face floating just out of reach, Andrew remembered their conversation at lunch. She had *wanted* to tell him, but she couldn't. Did she suspect who the person was who threatened her? Then why not say? Or was it all too vague to pin down?

Andrew walked back and forth, along the path to the stone bench and back to the arbor, torn with anxiety. Was it actually nothing at all? Had the shock of being the cause of her husband's death, no matter how unintended, loosened her hold on reality? Having come so close to death herself, perhaps any voice or footstep might loom as something ominous. But much as he wanted to believe this, he couldn't see Tina going into hiding—which, obviously, she had—on the strength of such insubstantial fear.

Turning at last into the house, he heard voices in the entry hall and saw Luigi speaking with a dark-haired man, telling him the signora had gone away.

Seeing Andrew, the man turned to him, black eyes burning. "You must be Dr. Quentin?" His English was accented but precise.

"Yes."

"I am Carlo Renzi." There was no offer of a handshake, only a cold glare. "I hear my cousin has gone away."

His cousin? Then Andrew remembered that Italians often make no in-law distinctions. As his cousin's wife, Carlo would regard Tina equally as his cousin.

"Yes, I believe she left this afternoon."

With a searing glance at the old servant, Carlo said,

"Luigi seems to know nothing. Do *you* know where she has gone?"

"No, I'm afraid not."

"Or for how long?"

"No."

"This is stupid. We have many papers to sign, many problems to solve before Mario's estate can be settled. Why should she run off? It is not, how do you say, responsible."

Andrew said nothing, returning Carlo's scrutiny with a noncommittal look. The brief battle of the eyes ended with Carlo giving a contemptuous shrug and instructing Luigi to tell the signora to speak with him the moment she returned.

Back in his study, Andrew wrenched his mind away from concern for Tina and moved to the piano, where that morning he had been working with undisturbed concentration on passages from Marini's opera, *Christabel*.

In the opera, first performed in 1940, Marini and his librettist had created an ending for Coleridge's uncompleted poem, "Christabel." In the early years of the nineteenth century, poor Coleridge had failed to say no to drugs and had inadvertently become addicted to opium. Scholarly battles on this issue apart, it seemed only too likely that his failure to finish some of his works was a result of this addiction, as well as of his own dilatory nature.

In the case of "Christabel," the magic of the poetry had survived all obstacles, and the fact that the poem breaks off at a frustrating moment of crisis had provided the chance for speculation on its possible conclusions.

Set in a mythical medieval kingdom, the poem

begins with Christabel, the daughter of Sir Leoline, kneeling in a forest, praying for her absent lover. There she finds a beautiful but mysterious woman named Geraldine, whom she befriends. Soon the innocent Christabel, who has caught terrifying glimpses of Geraldine's evil eye, falls under a spell cast by the sorceress, but meanwhile Papa has become enamored of the lady and will hear no complaints against her. Just as the lovely Christabel falls on her knees and begs her father to send the woman away, and Sir Leoline rejects his beloved daughter in favor of the enchanting Geraldine, the poem breaks off.

Andrew had always liked the ending created by Marini and his librettist, in which Geraldine puts Christabel into a deathlike trance, intending for her to be buried alive in the family tomb. Christabel's father's grief is matched by that of the lover, who, like Romeo, returns to find his beloved apparently dead. Not the least of its merits was the opportunity this libretto gave Marini to write the memorable music of the lament, with its impressive chorus and funeral procession, as well as the triumphant love duet when the young man unravels the plot and is reunited with his Christabel.

While not performed as often as the Verdi and Puccini favorites, Marini's opera still turned up from time to time in opera houses around the world, and it was scheduled for a performance in London in early November. In fact, Andrew's original intention had been to remain here in Florence until late October, going over to London in time for the performance of *Christabel* at the English National Opera at the Coliseum.

Now, he realized, everything depended on Tina. If she was in any kind of danger, he would remain, even if she didn't ask for his help. *I may not be a medieval* knight in armor, he thought wryly, but I can at least stick around and keep an eye on her.

With a breath that came from deep in his chest, he turned back to the papers on his desk.

• 7 •

AFTER TINA'S ABRUPT DEPARTURE, ANDREW FORCED HIM-self to concentrate on his work, finding it hard to exorcise the vision of her pale face as he had last seen her in the deep-sea cavern of the dining room.

The next morning, he dropped his note cards in disgust and wandered disconsolately into the kitchen to watch Anna making tortellini. As she flattened the dough and deftly twisted the small shapes, he looked on in silence, glad she tolerated his presence.

Soon after his arrival at Casa Marini, when he had made his first visit to the kitchen to express his pleasure in Anna's cuisine, she had stood stiffly before him, hands folded over her stomach, frowning as Tina had warned him she would do. Muttering, *"Grazie, signore,"* she had turned to one side in a dismissive gesture, and Andrew had duly retreated. However, on a second try, some days later, Anna had surveyed him, her black eyes filmed with age, and gestured toward a high stool.

"You've made a hit with Anna," Tina had said, amused. "She's like a cat. A few rare beings meet with her approval. The rest are as dust."

Now Andrew lolled on his familiar perch on a stool in the kitchen, one foot on the floor, the other hooked over a rung of the stool, studying Anna. Despite gray hair springing out of the careless knot at the back of her head, feet in loose slippers, print dress splotched with flour and oil, lined face set in its habitual scowl, she had a dignity that was lacking in her husband Luigi, with his emotional exclamations and gestures.

After a suitable period of silence, Andrew made an opening gambit with a question about the health of a grandchild who had been reported ill in their last halting conversation. Not always able to understand all of Anna's rapid speech, he nevertheless got the gist of her reply, responding that he was pleased to hear the little boy had recovered.

His Italian never failed to amuse Anna, drawing from her the tolerant look one might bestow on the efforts of a small child first learning to speak. She never corrected his speech, but would sometimes shake her head in pity that a man so learned seemed to know so little. Andrew, enjoying this game as much as Anna did, often attempted phrases beyond his powers just to see that flash of her eyes break into her usual solemnity.

Now, the daily cleaner appeared to ask Anna a question, and the two women spoke vehemently in the Tuscan dialect, with Anna hurling *"Stupido"* after the woman as she flounced away.

After another interval of silence and a few desultory exchanges with Anna, Andrew hazarded a reference to Tina. "The signora will return soon, *è vero?"*

Anna's filmy black eyes looked sharply into his, her hands frozen in midair. "I know nothing of the signora or her plans."

Undeterred, Andrew went on, "Signor Carlo Renzi came to ask for her."

Now the scowl covered her face and she punched the dough in silence. Carlo was evidently not one of her favorites. Feeling he had pushed his luck far enough, Andrew cheerfully whistled a tune from Verdi, and with a word of appreciation for yesterday's fagioli, sauntered out of the kitchen.

An hour later, remembering Tina's friend, Susie Brecht, the blond young woman in shorts he had met on the terrace, Andrew asked Luigi for a telephone book and found an S. J. Brecht on a street not far from the Ponte Vecchio.

A man's voice answered *"Pronto"*, and then Susie came on the phone. "Of course I remember you!" she exclaimed, when Andrew identified himself. "What's new?"

Feeling like a fool, Andrew asked if she happened to know where Tina had gone.

"Gone? Isn't she there?"

"No. She left yesterday, quite suddenly."

"Doesn't Luigi know where she went?"

"No, she didn't say."

Another pause. Then, "Look, Andrew, why don't you come down here?"

"I'd like that very much."

"Good. Got something to write on?"

And Susie gave him directions for finding her apartment.

A climb up five flights of stairs brought Andrew to Susie's door.

"Hi! Come on in."

Susie led the way to a small balcony garden, ringed with potted plants, the creamy stucco and red tile roofs of the surrounding buildings warm in the October sun.

Handing Andrew a mug of coffee, Susie said, "Here,

sit down. Alex's going off on a sketching trip. He's out picking up some stuff, but he'll be back in a minute. So, what's this about Tina? Why didn't she say where she was going?"

"I don't know, Susie. I hoped you would have some idea."

"Not a clue. But look, you're really worried, I can see that. So what's the problem?"

Andrew hesitated. "I don't know how much I should say."

Her blue eyes suddenly alert, Susie leaned forward. "Look, Andrew, Tina and I have no secrets from each other. If she was in trouble, she would have told me. So it's probably nothing."

"That's what I hope."

"Wait a minute—yesterday? We were gone all day yesterday. Maybe she tried to call me. When did she leave?"

"In the afternoon. We had lunch together . . ." Andrew swallowed.

"And she told you something, didn't she? What was it?"

"She said she thought her life was in danger."

"Oh, my God! And then she went away?"

"Yes. She had a suitcase, and told Anna she didn't know how long she'd be gone."

Susie stood up and leaned against the balustrade, looking down at the street below. Then she turned back to Andrew, her mouth twisted slightly, half amused, half commiserating. "The old black magic's got to you, has it?"

Intending an immediate denial, he looked at Susie's lightly freckled face, with its open and downright frankness, and threw in the towel.

"Yes, it looks that way."

"I'm not surprised. Tina is pretty devastating."

"Yes, she's lovely." Andrew was astonished to find how eager he was to acknowledge his passion.

"And what about Tina?"

"Oh, she sees me as a friend, I think."

"Hmm. Now, tell me exactly what she said to you before she left."

"She said it sounded crazy but she thought someone was trying to kill her."

"That was all she said? She didn't tell you what had happened?"

"No. She said she wanted to tell me but she couldn't."

"Hmm. There must have been specific threats: phone calls, letters, someone following her?"

"Yes, but she didn't tell me. So, who would stand to gain from her death? I see why that's the classic question, because it *is* the first thing that comes to mind."

"Exactly. Well, Carlo for one. I'm sure he'd get the lion's share of Mario's estate with Tina out of the way. Then there's Edmund and Mamma Emilia, as nice a pair of vultures as you'd want to meet. On the other hand, leaving out the money, there's the old crime of passion. Luisa was pretty steamed up the other day about Tina being responsible for Mario's death."

"Yes, I remember."

"Then there was the guy she had an affair with last year. Sorry, Andrew, but we might as well face facts."

"It's all right. She told me there had been some-one—"

"Right. But since they broke up ages ago, I can't see him suddenly turning homicidal at this point."

"No."

Hearing the scrape of feet on the stairs, Susie said,

"That's Alex. He doesn't need to know about Tina, okay? Let's go inside. It's getting hot out here."

A fist pounded on the door and a voice shouted, "Sus—*ee!*"

"Coming!"

As Andrew dropped into a low chair in a corner of the room, Susie released the double locks and opened the door to what looked, to Andrew's eyes—still blurred from the bright sun of the roof garden—like a black bear.

As the door shut behind him, the bear growled and clutched Susie to its chest. Presently, human hands moved down her body and the blond head detached itself from the black one.

"Hold it, Alex—someone's here."

"Aw, sheet!"

Laughing, Susie said, "Andrew, this is Alex," and the bear grunted and flopped onto the sofa, stretching out jean-clad legs and propping sandaled feet on a foot stool.

"Andrew's the professor who's writing a life of Tina's father."

As the black head swiveled in Andrew's direction, two brown eyes and a red mouth were visible in the enveloping shag. "Cool, man, cool."

Susie giggled. "Alex thinks all Americans talk like that."

Curling up in the only remaining chair, Susie said, "How about a beer, Andrew?"

"Sounds good."

Alex nodded. "For me also."

Susie waited a full beat, then looked levelly at Alex. "In the fridge, buddy boy. Make it three."

"Comin' up!" Alex bounded to his feet and started for the kitchen.

Susie said, "He's crazy about 'weemen's leeb.' Of

course, it's the novelty that appeals. We've only been together six months."

"Nothing serious, then?"

"Are you kidding? No way."

Halfway through their beers, Alex bounced up again, saying to Andrew, "You want to see my work? You buy something, maybe?" And he led Andrew into a small room where the light from a single window didn't do much to dispel the dusk. An easel stood at the ready, canvases leaned three or four deep against the walls, and two shelves displayed a surprisingly tidy collection of paints, brushes, and paraphernalia.

"Can you paint in this light?" Andrew asked.

"No, not like this." Alex pressed a switch, flooding the room with artificial light. "You think there must be big attic with north windows, eh? That's a load of sheet."

Like a salesman in a shop, Alex placed one painting after another on the easel. Expecting the usual blobs and streaks of contemporary art, Andrew saw instead a series of quite recognizable scenes of Florence, though not the standard views of the cathedral or the shop-lined bridge of the Ponte Vecchio. Done with a certain flair, the paintings were not Raphael or Andrea del Sarto, but not bad in their way.

"I paint from the roof—come, I show you."

Now Andrew saw that many of the rooftops and the glimpses of the river or the tower of the Palazzo Vecchio in Alex's paintings were done from different angles of the balcony garden.

"Is good, eh? At art school in Athens everybody want to be avant-garde, but I say, is fine for ones who cannot draw. I like to draw, and I like to sell. Not to want money is sheet. There is shop here that sells my stuff, but if you want to buy from me, will save you money."

"Thanks, Alex. I'll give it some thought."

"Cool, man."

Back in the sitting room, Alex swallowed the last of his beer and shouldered a backpack that had been standing in the corner. "Gotta go now. Back in a few days. See you later, alligator."

With a long kiss for Susie, he was gone.

$$\bullet \ 8 \ \bullet$$

ON SATURDAY, THE FOURTH DAY AFTER TINA HAD GONE, Susie phoned Andrew, as she had done each day, to ask for news of Tina.

"No, nothing."

"Come on down and we'll worry together."

Over coffee in Susie's apartment, they talked about calling the police and agreed it would be useless since they had nothing to go on, no evidence of threats, and no clue as to where Tina might be.

Changing the subject, Andrew asked if she had heard from Alex.

"No. He'll turn up when he's ready. He likes to wander around till he finds a place that suits him. Then he'll work like a beaver, with no thought of time."

The raucous sound of a buzzer came out of the wall, and Susie went to the intercom and pressed the button.

"Yes?"

Crackling sounds and a man's voice.

Then Susie said, *"Edmund?* Yes, of course, come on up."

She pressed the release for the entry door to the building.

"Edmund must have come looking for Tina. Did she tell you he's lost a packet of money again?"

"Yes. Actually, I was there when he telephoned."

"The idiot. Probably conned by some chap wearing an old school tie. All the Trahernes go to Eton. Tina said she refused to help him, and I don't blame her. She bailed him out several years ago, but right now her own affairs are tied up until Mario's estate is settled, and besides, Edmund ought to know better."

"By the way, Susie, I'm not sure Tina's mother knows I'm staying at the house—"

"I know, but it's too late now. Edmund will of course stay at Casa Marini while he's here in the city. After all, it's Emilia's house, and they lived there off and on for years. So no problem—you're a scholar using the annex for a short time, that's all."

As Susie opened the door of the flat and stood waiting, Andrew could hear ascending footsteps and a man's voice protesting, "Such a climb! Dear me, I'm quite out of breath!"

Susie said, without enthusiasm, "Come in, Edmund."

"Thank you, my dear child, thank you. You're looking lovely, as always."

With a quick upward roll of her eyes at Andrew as he stood up, Susie merely said, "This is Dr. Andrew Quentin, from California. Edmund Traherne."

"How d'you do? A pleasure."

Edmund shook hands, then subsided into a chair. In spite of the heat, Edmund's short, trim body was clad in flannels and a double-breasted blazer, a diamond pin nestling in his silk ascot. With his silver hair, aquamarine eyes, and an even-featured face with fair, transparent skin, Edmund would have been a handsome man for his age had it not been for the cherry red pouches under his eyes and the deep carmine of the cheeks and nose.

"Would you like a beer, Edmund?"

"Have you a gin and tonic, my dear?"

"Yes, there should be some around the place. With ice?"

"Yes, please!"

As Susie departed for the kitchen, Edmund turned to Andrew. "You Americans are so right about ice. We used to sniff at it, but now half our friends won't take a drink without it. I simply adore Americans. Is this your first visit to Italy?"

"No, I've been here a number of times."

"I see. Splendid. Are you on holiday?"

"No. My field is music. I'm doing some research on Piero Marini."

Edmund's brows shot up. "Then you've met his daughter Cristina?"

As Susie returned with Edmund's drink, Andrew said casually, "Yes. She suggested I might use the annex at Casa Marini while I am here."

Edmund blinked, then said cheerfully, "Yes, why not? No one's used it in donkey's years."

Andrew noted with relief that Edmund didn't seem to share Mamma Emilia's objection to research on the composer.

Now Susie asked Edmund, "How's Emilia?"

"Coming along splendidly. Her speech is improving day by day, and the doctors say she may come home in a few days. Of course, she will be in the wheelchair for some time, as walking is difficult still."

"Is she in good spirits?"

Edmund paused, then went smoothly on. "Yes, under the circumstances, yes indeed. It's been a most trying experience for her, as one can well imagine."

Draining his glass, Edmund looked toward the kitchen. "May I just top this up? Save you the trouble."

"Help yourself."

When he was gone, Susie held up thumb and forefinger wide apart, indicating to Andrew the size of drink Edmund was no doubt pouring for himself. Then she murmured, "Emilia's the all-time bitch. It'll be fun and games for Edmund when she comes home."

Returning with a well-filled glass, Edmund sat down and crossed his legs in their sharply creased flannels. "So, Susan, where has our little Tina gone? Luigi tells me she left no word."

"I don't know, Edmund. She didn't leave a message for me either."

"It's most distressing. I spoke with her on the phone the other day, and she said nothing about going away. I need to consult with her about a little matter, so I decided to pop over while Emilia is still in hospital."

"I'm afraid I can't help you."

"I can wait over until Monday, but then I shall have to return."

In the ensuing silence, Edmund took another generous swig of his drink, then looked at Andrew genially.

"Dr. Quentin, I expect you've heard that Marini's opera *Christabel* is scheduled soon for the ENO in London?"

"Yes, I'm planning to be there."

"Splendid! Emilia is desperately anxious to be able to attend, even if she must go in the wheelchair. She's to be presented with a plaque of some sort before the curtain. Then we shall be giving a reception after the performance."

Susie asked, "What about Tina? Is she included in the presentation?"

Edmund's aquamarine eyes darted to one side. "Possibly, possibly. They may have thought she would not wish to come all the way from Italy."

With heavy irony, Susie said, "I wonder where they would get that idea?"

"And of course, with the recent death of her husband, I should think Cristina would not be ready for public appearances. By the by, how *did* Mario die? We saw a rather garbled account in the news that Cristina had killed him herself, although she tells us he attacked her."

"It was an accident, Edmund. It's all settled now."

"So she told Emilia on the telephone. Splendid, splendid!"

Swallowing the last of his drink, Edmund rose. "I must be off, then. Thank you, my dear!"

Andrew stood up. "May I give you a lift?"

"No, no, dear boy, I shall be spending the evening with friends here in town. I expect I'll see you later on at the Casa. Good-bye, good-bye!"

When the door closed behind Edmund, Susie giggled. "What a phony! He never changes."

"You know him well, I gather."

"Oh, lord yes. Tina and I spent a lot of our school holidays together at my family's place on the Hudson or with Emilia and Edmund, either here or in the Lake Country. Later on, in college days, we managed to go off more on our own after the obligatory home visits. Edmund always oozes on as if I'm Miss America, but it's just his way. His only plus, in my opinion, is that he's devoted to Emilia. There's never been any hanky-panky, so far as I know."

"Would Tina's mother actually try to prevent her daughter from coming to the opera first-night event?"

Susie laughed. "Like a shot. Emilia likes to queen it as the widow of the great composer, and she doesn't want any competition from his gorgeous daughter. There's no love lost between those two, I can tell you!"

"How tragic that Tina lost her father."

"Yes. Only ten years old. She absolutely worshiped him. When I first knew her, only a few months after he died, she couldn't talk about it at all. Then she would have crying fits in the night. Some of the girls at school made fun of her, but I used to sit on the edge of her bed and hold her hand till she stopped sobbing. And we've been friends ever since."

"Marini's biographers seem to agree that his death was accidental, but I've never understood exactly how it happened. He went out late at night on the jetty where the small boat was kept, but they say he never went out in the boat because he hadn't learned to swim and was terrified of the water. Yet he was sitting on a wooden bench at the end of the jetty, and somehow he fell and was drowned."

"Yes, that's all I know about it too. Tina thought she heard the splash, and ran down through the garden to the edge of the lake, but by the time she went for help, it was too late. Poor child! That was her recurring nightmare—that he was simply gone, and she never saw him again until his body was recovered from the lake."

"But how could he have fallen in if he was so cautious about the water? I wondered if he had had a heart attack, but according to the sources, the post-mortem gave no indication of it."

"Maybe something frightened him, causing him to jump back and accidentally fall."

"Yes, but what?"

"I suppose we'll never know."

• 9 •

ANDREW HAD BEEN BACK AT HIS DESK AT CASA MARINI FOR an hour or so when Luigi summoned him to the telephone.

"Andrew, it's Jane! Would you believe—I'm flying into Pisa tomorrow! Are you going to be around? I'll take the train into Florence—"

"No. Never mind the train. What time is your flight? I have my car. I'll meet you at the airport!"

And so it was arranged. Jane Winfield, his former graduate student at their university in California, now living in London with her solicitor husband, James Hall, had become one of Andrew's most valued friends. Having directed Jane's doctoral dissertation on a nineteenth century English composer, he had collaborated with her the following year on a biography which was still selling well. In his frequent visits to London, Andrew had become a welcome member of the Hall household and an honorary uncle to their infant daughter.

Jane, now a free-lance writer, had recently finished a book on a world-renowned pianist and was regularly engaged as a music critic for various periodicals in London. It was this activity that had brought her on short notice to Italy.

At the Pisa airport the next morning Jane emerged from customs, dropped her briefcase and carryon bag, and threw her arms around Andrew. "I can't believe my luck! It's great enough to be given this trip, but to see you here too—it's fabulous!"

"So how did it happen?"

"His nibs tripped on the stairs and sprained his ankle."

Correctly interpreting this as a reference to the chief music reviewer of a popular London magazine, Andrew said, "Too much vino again?"

"Yes, I suspect so. Anyhow, it's a break for me. *Arts Weekly* had set up this trip for him to cover the new production of *Nabucco* at La Scala, and as their unofficial second string, I fell heir to it. I asked them to book me through here, and I'll take the train to Milan tomorrow."

As Andrew drove out of the small airport, he asked, "So, how are James and the *bellissima bambina?*"

"Thriving! She loves the music box you sent for her birthday! By the way, this trip held another bonus for me. James had promised his mother to bring Laura down to Devon for her first birthday and spend a few days there. When this came up, I was able to make a graceful escape."

"Mrs. Hall hasn't warmed up to you yet?"

Jane giggled. "No, I get tight-lipped remarks about young mothers who leave their babies with housekeepers. She ignores the fact that I'm at home most of the time. Besides, my dear housekeeper is a better granny to Laura than my sainted mother-in-law will ever be."

"I can believe that. Grim is the word that springs to my lips in my recollections of Mrs. Hall."

"Exactly. She adores James, but she only tolerates me—she still hasn't forgiven me for not producing a boy."

As they approached the town of Pisa, Andrew said, "Want to stop at the cathedral?"

Jane's expressive brown eyes flashed approval. "Yes, please! I was there with my father years ago, in my school days. Let's just stand at the gate and gaze."

"Good idea. We'll never be able to park on a Sunday morning during mass."

Following the signs posted for tourists to the Piazza dei Miracoli, Andrew drew up by the entrance to the cathedral square. Waved back by a traffic warden, he called out *"Un momento"* and gestured for Jane to step out. Through the windshield he could see the gleaming white marble of the baptistery, the cathedral itself, and beyond it, the leaning tower, radiant in the October sunlight. Despite the autumn drought, the extensive lawns had been tended to keep their jewel-like green.

He watched as Jane stood in the gateway, her soft brown hair lifted by a light breeze. What a darling she was. If only Tina would turn up today, so Jane could meet her. Five days now since Tina disappeared. Pain, like a living creature, tugged in his chest and swelled his throat.

Jane, getting back into the car, said with fervor, "Gorgeous! I'm glad we stopped."

"They're not allowing people to climb the tower now—too dangerous."

Jane smiled. "So I've heard. When I came with my father, I must have been about fourteen. We explored the baptistery and wandered all around the cathedral, and the poor darling must have been dreading having to climb the tower, because when I said I didn't want to go up, he positively beamed and said, 'Wonderful! Let's go and have lunch.'"

"Speaking of lunch, I've got an agenda, if it's all right with you. The cook at Casa Marini said to bring you back for a meal. You won't regret it—she would get some stars from Michelin if she went public. And

Susie Brecht invited us to meet for coffee at five o'clock."

An hour later, in the green gloom of the dining room at Casa Marini, Jane had her first sample of Anna's genius, a pasta of indefinable delicacy.

"Mmm, I see what you mean. I suppose I should learn to be a gourmet cook, but it's so much easier to let someone else do it."

On the drive into the city, Andrew had brought Jane up to date on his research on Piero Marini, and then poured out the story of Tina, from the accidental death of her husband to her subsequent disappearance.

Quietly, Jane had said, "You care for her very much, don't you?"

And Andrew had said simply, "Yes, very much."

"And Tina?"

"I don't know."

Now, seeing Jane in the very chair in which Tina had sat on the day she went away, Andrew felt a stab of anguish. "Somehow, I was sure she would come back today. I don't know why."

Jane pondered. "Have you heard any more from the cousin—Carlo?"

"No, not since he came blustering and complaining on the afternoon she left."

"And what about Edmund Traherne?"

"Oh lord, I nearly forgot about Edmund. He must be staying here at the house, but I didn't see him this morning. Still, if there had been any word from Tina, Luigi would have told me."

After lunch Andrew led the way to the kitchen, where Jane thanked Anna with an unassuming friendliness that drew a nod and a *"Grazie, signora."*

Then, in the annex, the two spent several hours poring over the cache of Marini material, Andrew bringing out each special treasure like a proud parent, playing passages on the piano or giving them to Jane to run through.

"Here's a gem," he said, playing the Coleridge song, "Answer to a Child's Question," as Jane bent over his shoulder and sang the words.

"I love the ending," she exclaimed. "Do the last lines again."

When Andrew came to some early versions of themes from the opera, *Christabel*, Jane exclaimed, "By the way, great news! *Arts Weekly* has given me the whole assignment for the London production next month. Not just the opening night review, but feature articles as well. I hope to get an interview with the second wife, Emilia—your Tina's mother—and I'm going up to Keswick in a few days to check out the local scene and look up the first wife, Vera."

Andrew nodded. "She's in her eighties, isn't she? Pave the way for me if you get to see her, as I certainly want to interview her later on if I can. Up to now I've spent most of my time in the libraries, working through all the critical material on Marini. Now I'm ready to start digging into his personal life, including the curious circumstances of his death."

"Tina was a child when he died, wasn't she?"

"Yes, ten years old."

Andrew reported what he had heard of Marini's death.

Jane said, "You think it might have been murder?"

"I don't know, but it's possible."

Then Jane echoed Susie Brecht's words. "Mmm. I suppose we'll never know what really happened."

When Jane had checked into her hotel in the old part of the city, Andrew said, "Let's walk from here. Finding a parking place was a miracle, even on a Sunday. We won't press our luck."

In the nearly perfect weather they joined the Sunday afternoon strollers, and in ten minutes or so had reached the Piazza Signoria, the central square of the old town, where a water-stained copy of Michelangelo's David stood near the entrance to the Uffizi Gallery.

Across the square they found the café designated by Susie, who had reported that Alex was back.

Jane looked at her watch. "Five o'clock. Are you sure this is the place?"

Andrew grinned. "Time means nothing in Italy, you may remember. They'll be along. Let's have a cappuccino."

Sitting at an outdoor table, they looked across the square at the contrasting styles of the buildings—the severe brown stone of the thirteenth century Palazzo Vecchio, the Renaissance elegance of the Uffizi beyond it, and to the right, the graceful arches of the Loggia.

Twenty minutes later, when Susie and Alex strolled in, Andrew made the introductions, then looked eagerly at Susie. "Any word from Tina?"

"No, nothing."

"I've told Jane."

Susie said, "Glad you're here, Jane. Andrew needs a friend."

"Only till tomorrow, I'm afraid."

The four chatted amiably over their coffee, Susie surprising Andrew by insisting on seeing a picture of Jane's baby.

Susie handed Alex the snapshot. "Look, isn't she a love?"

Alex beamed. "You want baby? I give you baby, then we get married, yes?"

"Oops—no!" Susie grinned. "Sorry, Alex. I'll have to find a steady provider before I launch into motherhood."

Alex nodded cheerfully. "Right on, babe!"

Jane put Laura's picture back in her handbag and gazed out at the paved surface of the huge square. "I see the anti-archeology group won the battle."

Andrew said, "Yes. Last time I was here, at least half the square was taken up with the dig. The combat must have been fierce."

Susie grimaced. "The Florentines were practically

split into armed camps—the march of science versus the preservation of the city, and so on."

"I must say, the excavation did look odd in the middle of a famous historic piazza."

"Yes. I doubt if the Romans would have dug up great chunks of the square of St. Peter's!"

By seven o'clock they had switched to drinks and decided to go on to dinner together, when Andrew looked up and saw Edmund Traherne approaching their table, walking with the care of a man who is none too sure of his balance.

"Good evening, dear children!" Edmund's voice was gravelly, and little beads of perspiration dotted his forehead. "May I join you?"

"Of course."

Presented to Jane, Edmund engaged in some London chitchat, pausing only to order a double gin and tonic.

Then, his aquamarine eyes darting from one face to another, he asked, "Is there any news of our little Tina?"

At their negative replies, Edmund downed half his drink and sighed. "Very naughty of her to run off like this. Oh, dear, how warm it is!"

Actually, the evening air was cool, but Edmund fumbled in the pocket of his flannels, pulling out a handkerchief. Something dropped with a thud, and Andrew, bending to pick up the object, found himself holding a knife encased in tooled Florentine leather.

As he stared at the knife, Alex reached across the table and took it in his hands, pulling it out to reveal a beautifully jeweled handle and a wicked-looking steel blade.

"Is sharp!" Alex pulled back the finger with which he had touched the edge of the weapon.

Susie said, "Edmund, what on earth are you doing with that thing?"

Now Andrew saw that the usual blotches of red on Edmund's face had spread in a crimson tide from neck to silver hairline.

"It's just a little thing I picked up in a shop, my dear."

Slurping the last of his drink, Edmund put the sheathed knife back in his pocket and stood up, bending toward Jane. "Delighted to meet you, my dear young lady. Do come to us in Hampstead! I must be off. Good-bye!"

Susie sniffed. "If he bought the knife in a shop, why is he carrying it around in his pocket?"

Two more days of agony ensued for Andrew before Tina came back. On Monday, Jane had taken the train to Milan, and Edmund Traherne had flown back to London. Susie and Alex left town for a few days, leaving a number in Ravenna for Andrew to ring if he heard from Tina.

On Tuesday night, unable to sleep, Andrew had wandered out to the darkness of the terrace and sunk into a chair. Throughout the week, a welcome rain had cooled the air and freshened the parched countryside. Andrew sat staring gloomily at the water that still dripped from the barren grape vines over the arbor, when he heard voices in the house behind him. On his feet, heart thudding, he heard Luigi exclaiming noisily and Tina telling Luigi to take her bag up to her bedroom. Then the door to the terrace opened and Tina said softly, "Andrew?"

"Yes, I'm here."

He reached her in two strides and pulled her against him, uttering his relief in hoarse whispers. "You're safe—Tina, I've been frantic!"

Her head against his chest, Tina murmured, "You do care, don't you?"

"You know I do."

She raised both hands and caressed his face, looking up at him intently. "You're a lovely man, Andrew," she whispered, and turned back to the house.

Half an hour later Andrew sat up in bed, watching occasional shafts of moonlight come through the half-shuttered windows and make barred patterns on the wall. Hearing a tap on the door that led to the terrace, he threw on a robe and found Tina standing there.

"I couldn't sleep," she said simply.

He drew her into the room, holding her against him, feeling her arms go around his neck. Kissing her eyes, her lips, moving his hands down her body over her clinging negligee, he felt, along with the surge of physical desire, a sense of well-being, something that said, This is what I've waited for.

Then at last Andrew found himself speaking the words he hadn't been able to say to any woman since his wife died.

"I love you, Tina. You know that, don't you?"

The lowest of whispers. "Yes."

Now Tina let her gown drop to the floor. Her dark eyes looking into his, her mouth curving in the near smile of the San Miniato madonna, she slid her arms under his robe.

• 10 •

THE TOWN OF KESWICK, IN ENGLAND'S LAKE DISTRICT, lies in a valley surrounded by sharp, barren peaks, a quarter of a mile from Derwentwater, one of the loveliest of the lakes.

On the Wednesday of the week following her visit to Italy, Jane Winfield took an afternoon train from London to Penrith and caught a local bus into Keswick. From the bus station at the bottom of the hill, she followed directions up the high street to the hotel where she was booked for two nights. A sharp wind swept gray clouds across the sky, while shafts of sunlight fitfully turned buildings and treetops pale yellow until eclipsed by the onrushing gloom.

The hotel offered welcome warmth, as Jane signed the register and was shown up a short flight of stairs, along a passage, through two more turnings and several fire doors, before reaching her room. Now that she was here, the fatigue of the day evaporated. Adept at traveling light, she unpacked her single over-the-shoulder bag and took out the phone number of Vera Marini.

A local girl whom Piero Marini had met when he first came to the Lake District in the 1930s, Vera now lived in the house that had been her parents' home since her childhood. Her marriage to Marini had lasted only eight years, and after their divorce, she had lived chiefly in London before returning to Keswick to spend her last days. There had been a son, Clifford, from a previous marriage, about whom very little was known, except that the child had not lived with Vera and Marini during their marriage, coming only for visits to his mother.

After several double rings to Vera's number, Jane heard a man's voice on the line. "Yes?"

"Mrs. Vera Cox, please."

"Who is speaking?" The voice was anything but cordial.

"My name is Jane Winfield, with *Arts Weekly* in London. I am here in Keswick now, and I'm ringing to confirm my appointment with Mrs. Cox for tomorrow."

"I'm not at all sure Mrs. Cox is available."

Now Jane could hear a woman's voice. "Who is it, dear?"

"Some journalist from London, Mother. Sounds like a Yank. I'll tell her to go away."

"No, Clifford. Tell her to come, in the morning."

"Oh, very well. Miss, er, you may come at ten o'clock tomorrow, if you like."

"Thank you very much."

So that was Clifford. Not a forthcoming subject, but fortunately she didn't need to interview *him*. Marini's opera, *Christabel,* had been written in 1939, during his marriage to Vera. At that date Clifford had been a child of four, hardly old enough to have a significant contribution to make.

Pleased at her appointment for the morning, Jane looked out the window, catching a passing blip of sunshine. Plenty of time to do some exploring before dark. Putting on jeans, a warm jersey, walking boots, and her hooded jacket, she stuffed some money in a pocket and set off.

Jane saw that Keswick, like other villages in the area, had kept its charm intact. Old-timers no doubt bewailed the modernized shop fronts and moaned about the traffic that clogged the roads all through the summer, but tourism, according to the guidebook she had brought along, remained the most profitable, and except for sheep-raising, almost the only industry in the Lake Country.

Wandering up the high street, looking in the shop windows, Jane found a tea shop and ordered a steaming pot and a toasted bun. Thus fortified, she decided there was time to have a look at Lakeside, the house Marini had bought before his marriage to Vera, and where he was staying at the time of his death.

Finding a taxi, she asked the driver if he could take her to Lakeside.

"Do you mean the house where the musician fellow lived?"

"Yes."

"I can take you there right enough, but I don't think you'll find anyone about. Haven't seen any signs of life in quite a time."

"That's all right. I just want to have a look at the house."

As they drove out of the little town and down toward the lake, Jane had her first view of Derwentwater through a screen of trees now almost bare of leaves.

"It's lovely, isn't it?" she said.

"This your first visit to the district?" asked the driver, a friendly young man who told her his name was Nick.

"Not quite. I've been to Windermere, but not here at Keswick."

"American, are you?"

"Yes, but I live in London now."

Doing his duty as a tour guide, Nick said, "Windermere's the largest of the lakes, but this one's second—three miles long!"

Jane smiled, savoring the small-scale delights of her adopted country. Derwentwater might be only a pond by American standards, and the "fells" referred to as "mountains" might be mere foothills to the mighty ranges of the Rockies, but size alone was not the only criterion to charm the aesthetic senses.

After a mile or so along the road by the lake, Nick pointed to a large, rambling house of gray stone, the roof a jumble of steeply pitched gables of slate.

Following a narrow drive down through a patch of now leafless trees, he drew up before a back entrance to the house, which faced the lake on the other side.

Jane asked, "Can you wait here for a bit?"

"Take your time."

As Jane stepped out, pulling up the hood of her jacket against the wind, she heard the strains of pop music issuing from the cab as the driver settled back in his seat.

The sun had gone down some time before, and now Jane saw that the gray clouds were laced with black bands, darkening the already dusky light. Turning to her left, she began to circle the house, picking her way along a neglected gravel path, bordered with brownish shrubbery. Now the lake was in full view, and as she rounded the lower corner of the house, she could see the wooden jetty that extended out into the water, a bench at its end.

The hill on which the house was built had dropped sharply from the main road, but here the ground was almost level, sloping only slightly toward the water, the edge of the lake swampy with reeds. A veranda ran the full width of the house on this side, offering a fine view of a small island in the lake and of a craggy fell beyond.

About to turn away, Jane saw there was someone sitting on the bench, facing the lake. Suddenly the figure rose from the bench and stood still for a moment, a long black cloak covering the head and falling from the shoulders. Then the person sat down again, leaned forward, and lurched toward the water.

With a sharp gasp, Jane began to run across the coarse grass toward the jetty when the figure stood up again. Now the hood of the cloak fell back, disclosing a woman's long reddish hair falling halfway down her back.

Jane stopped and watched silently as the woman raised her arms, making wings of the black cloak, then dropped them and lowered her head.

Now she turned and walked slowly back along the jetty, the wind flapping the cloak against her body. Jane began to move back toward the house when she heard a voice call out, "Stop!"

Turning, she saw the woman striding toward her, the cloak flying behind her. A tall woman, she stood before Jane, large eyes glinting.

"Who are you? What are you doing here?"

The stare was mesmerizing.

"I'm a writer, from London. . . ."

The woman seemed not to hear, but her hand shot out and grasped Jane's arm. "He died out there. My Piero drowned in the lake."

Now Jane stared back. The woman must have been in her sixties. Even in the fading light Jane could see the gray in the auburn hair, and the lines in a face that had clearly once been of great beauty. Clearing her throat, she whispered, "Are you Geraldine?"

The huge eyes looked into Jane's. "Geraldine? Gerry. He always called me Gerry. But you see, he was afraid of the water."

"Yes, I know."

Now the eyes narrowed and the grip on Jane's arm tightened. "You? How could you know? You weren't there." The woman looked out toward the lake. "He's still out there, you know. They found his body, but my Piero's spirit is in the lake."

Jane stood silent as the woman looked down at her again.

"Maybe you can bring him back. He liked pretty young women like you. Yes, you can fetch him for me." With a sudden movement, the woman put her arm under Jane's knees and picked her up as easily as one might lift a child. Gripping Jane fiercely against her body, she strode onto the jetty muttering, "Yes, you can go in and bring him back. You can look for him in the lake. Piero, Piero—"

For a moment Jane's mind was blank with terror. Then she began to scream, kicking her feet against Geraldine's body. Would the taxi driver hear her? Not a chance, with his radio going full blast.

Now she tried to get the woman's attention. "Geraldine! Listen to me! Gerry! Put me down and I'll try to help you!"

But the woman was in another dimension, repeating her incantatory phrases.

Desperate, Jane freed her arms enough to raise both hands and grasp the woman's neck, pressing with her thumbs against the throat. At first there was no reaction. Then, just as they reached the end of the jetty, Geraldine stopped, dropping Jane's body as she reached for the hands that were around her throat. Jane let go and kicked at the woman's shins, but before she could get her balance, Geraldine pushed both hands against Jane's waist and flung her over the end of the jetty, into the water.

· 11 ·

APART FROM SHEER TERROR, JANE'S FIRST SENSATION AS she plunged into the waters of the lake was of pulse-stopping cold. Knowing that the water will be cold is no preparation for the reality, she learned. Holding her breath as she fell, she still couldn't avoid a sharp gasp as the chill swept through her body. Choking, eyes and mouth filled with water, she kicked vigorously and pushed down with her arms, desperate to breathe and terrified she wouldn't make it to the surface before another fatal intake of breath.

Then she could feel the upward rise of her body, and in a moment her head cleared the surface of the water. Now, with the relief of breathing, came more choking. Trying to tread water while she coughed and sputtered, she felt the pull of her boots as they filled with water.

As her breathing cleared, she shook the water out of her eyes, and looking around to get her bearings, saw only blackness. When she had been standing in the garden, there had still been enough light to see the house, the jetty, the manic glitter of Geraldine's eyes. But down here the dark surface of the water merged with the blackening sky.

Then, turning her head, she saw the outline of the jetty only a few yards away and struggled toward it. The floorboards were too high above her head to be reached, but she saw the rungs of a ladder on the far side of the jetty, and threw herself through the water till her hands grasped the first rung above the water line.

Weak with relief at having reached safety, she stopped only for a deep breath before seizing the next rung of the ladder, when she heard Gerry's voice crooning, "No, no, you must bring Piero—you must bring him back to me."

Looking up, Jane saw the black-cloaked figure kneeling at the end of the jetty, and as she began to pull herself up the ladder, the woman bent forward. Jane felt a sharp pain in the hand that held the upper rung of the ladder. Pulling it sharply away, she saw that Gerry held a flat stone, with which she now struck her other hand.

Recoiling from the pain of the blows, Jane grabbed for the lowest rung, out of the woman's reach, crying out, "No, Gerry, no. I'll help you get Piero back, but you must let me come up now. Please, Gerry—"

Unheeding, the moaning voice went on. "Piero, Piero . . ."

No earthly use in appealing to the poor woman, Jane thought. The only option was to strike off and try to reach the shore beyond the garden of Lakeside.

Knowing she couldn't swim for long encumbered with her jacket and boots, she let go of the ladder and pulled down on the zipper of the jacket. The zipper went down well enough, but at the bottom fastener it balked. Holding the ladder for a moment of respite, she took her hands away again and finally succeeded in freeing the jacket.

Now for the boots. Once they were off, she thought, she would slip out of the jacket and let it go.

Pausing, she looked in despair at the black surface of the lake. Even if she got rid of her boots and jacket, would she be able to swim far enough to reach the shore before the cold immobilized her? At home in California, she had always enjoyed casual swimming—a dip at the beach, a few laps in a pool—but swimming in the near dark in icy water was not something she wanted to put to the test.

Since there didn't seem to be much choice, she held the ladder with one hand and reached for a boot, trying to push down the zipper on the inner side. This was much stickier going than the zipper of the jacket had been, and harder to reach. She felt her breath coming in short gasps as she struggled—not a good sign, as she would need all the breath she could muster for the swim ahead.

Suddenly, she heard a masculine voice above her head.

"Here, give me your hand!"

The genial face of Nick, the taxi driver, loomed above her.

Thank God! But where was Geraldine?

As she pulled herself up the ladder, she heard Nick's voice again. "You, lady, take off your cloak. We're going to need it."

But a moment later, as the man's strong arms helped her onto the jetty, she saw the figure of Geraldine, black cloak flying, running through the garden and out of sight.

Putting his arm around Jane, Nick hurried her off to the taxi, where he turned up the heater and started the car.

"Who was the lady? Friend of yours?"

Jane made the instant decision that the story was far too bizarre to be explained. "No, she just happened to be there when I fell."

Nick's brows climbed toward his hairline, but he asked no further questions, and she left him with the impression she had leaned too far over the edge of the jetty and tumbled in.

At her hotel Nick helped her in, saying a friendly "Hello" to the young woman at the reception desk. "There's been an accident. Lady fell in the lake."

Jane fished a moist ten-pound note from her pocket and pressed it on the unwilling Nick, then accepted the offer of extra blankets from the hotel manager, ordered a drink to be sent up to her room, and at last sank into a hot bath.

Jane woke the next morning with a slight sniffle, but otherwise unharmed by her dip in the lake; except, she reflected, that it hadn't done much for her confidence as a swimmer.

Musing over the madness that had obviously overtaken poor Geraldine Foster, she wondered if her illness began at the time of her lover's death or if it had developed in later years, unconnected with the tragedy. Had there been signs of emotional imbalance during the time she had lived with Marini? Tina might know.

Thank heaven Tina was safe. Knowing Jane's concern, Andrew had telephoned her in London the day before to say that Tina had come back. His voice buoyant, he had said to her, "I've been humming the Coleridge song all morning!"

"I know what that means," Jane had reported to her husband James. "The last words of the song are 'My love loves me.'"

Having hoped for years that a new love would come along for Andrew, to help ease the pain of his wife's death, Jane was ecstatic.

"And he found her without any help from you, darling," James had teased.

"You're so right. I don't have to engage in any more matchmaking."

"Did Andrew say anything about Tina's fear that someone was threatening her life?"

"No. That must mean that whatever it was, it's all right now. And good news—Tina's coming to London for the opening night of the opera. I can't wait to meet her!"

Without mentioning it to Andrew, Jane had wondered if Tina might have come to the house here at Keswick to hide out from whatever was threatening her. But what Jane had seen of Lakeside that day had made it seem unlikely. The taxi driver had seen no signs of life for some time, and at this season, there would have to be lights at night and a fire for warmth if someone were living in the house.

The black clouds of the evening before had fulfilled their promise and produced a heavy downpour through the night, but gave up the ghost in the early morning, so that by a quarter of ten, when Jane set out for her interview with Vera Marini Cox, the weather was sullen but quiescent. Her jacket and boots were still too damp to wear, but with two sweaters, a wool skirt, a scarf over her head, and walking shoes, she felt comfortable enough.

Following directions given at the hotel, she walked up the sharp rise of the high street to the Borrowdale Road and presently found an attractive house which looked to be eighteenth century, with its pillared portico, white stucco walls, and black-framed windows.

Her ring was answered by a middle-aged woman in a striped coverall who said, "I'm Mabel," and showed Jane into a sitting room of classic Victorian clutter. China cabinets filled with bric-a-brac and little tables laden with vases and picture frames were dotted about in such profusion that Jane had to follow a zigzag path toward the hearth, where a gray-haired lady sat in a chair by the fire.

"Mrs. Cox! Miss Winfield's here." Mabel lowered her voice to Jane. "You'll want to speak up, miss. She's a bit hard of hearing."

The old lady looked up without rising. "That will do, Mabel. I'm not in the least deaf. Do sit down, Miss Winfield. Will you have coffee?"

"Yes, please."

When Mabel had gone, Jane said, "It's very good of you to see me, Mrs. Cox."

Vera Cox's lined face was impassive, but irony gleamed from her vivid blue eyes. "I expect it's something to do with Piero. I've had three husbands, Miss Winfield, and no one asks to see me about either of the others."

Jane smiled. "Yes. I've been asked to write some articles leading up to the new production of the opera *Christabel* in London. I believe the opera was composed during the time of your marriage to Mr. Marini."

Vera Cox threw her head back and looked at the ceiling. "Christabel. Yes, I was his Christabel."

There was a silence, then Vera lowered her head and looked at Jane. "You want to know what Piero was like, I expect. Yes. So long as Mr. Cox was alive, I refused to talk about Piero. Those chaps used to come 'round after Piero's death, writing books about him and asking questions, and I sent them away. My husband was very good to me, you see, and it wouldn't have done to give out my real feelings now, would it? But he died two years ago, and since I've come back here to Keswick, I've been haunted by those years with Piero."

Another silence, while Jane remained immobile. Then, on a breath, Vera said, "Piero was the most egocentric, self-centered creature who ever lived, but also the most tender, passionate, lovable of men. I adored him, hated him, was mesmerized by him. That's what he was like, Miss Winfield."

At this inauspicious moment Mabel arrived with a tray of coffee and biscuits, and Vera lapsed into innocuous remarks about the weather while Mabel handed the cups.

Sipping her coffee, Jane looked out of the window at the back garden of the house in time to see two figures walking along a path. One was an enormously fat man of middle age. Strands of gray hair circled a bald spot on the back of his head and formed a fringe that nestled into the roll of flesh at the base of his neck. The other was a tall, red-haired woman, and although Jane had only a glimpse of the pair before they moved out of sight, she wasn't likely to forget the face of Geraldine Foster, the madwoman at the lake.

• 12 •

OVER THE COFFEE CUPS, VERA COX LOOKED AT JANE WITH some curiosity.

"I believe you are an American, Miss Winfield?"

"Yes, but I live in London now with my husband and small daughter."

"I see. Then Winfield is your professional name?"

Jane smiled. "Yes. That often takes a bit of explaining."

"No, I quite understand. I was a singer for some

years, and I used my maiden name professionally. I sang a good deal during my first marriage, but with Piero, I sang very little."

"I'd have thought his prominence as a composer would have given you more opportunities—"

"No, no. Piero had no interest in my career. I doubt if he even thought of it as a career. I was twenty-nine when we married, and had had some good engagements, but I was not by any means in the first rank. It's impossible now to know how far I would have progressed, for when I met Piero, nothing else mattered to me. We met when my first husband and I were living in London and my little boy was only three years old."

Vera's vivid blue eyes studied Jane's face. "If I speak freely to you, it is because I believe I can trust you to observe discretion in what you write. Is that so?"

"Yes."

"Thank you. My son Clifford doesn't like for me to speak about the past, but I am eighty-one years old, and it is all so long ago, I can't see the harm in it now. You see, within a month of our first meeting, Piero and I became lovers. He simply wasn't the sort of man to wait for anything. When he saw something—or someone—he wanted, he seized it at once. I was bewitched by him. I've never loved any other man in that way.

"Piero was thirty-nine at the time—ten years older than I. He had had many liaisons but had never married. Now, he decided he wanted to marry and have a child—*our* child—and he assured me he was prepared to settle down and be an ideal family man. My husband agreed to the divorce—in fact, he secured it on the usual trumped-up grounds that were practiced in those days—but he refused to give up our son, nor would he allow the child to be taken out of England. Clifford might come for prescribed visits to me, but not in Italy.

"That was when Piero, knowing that my parents lived here in Keswick, explored the area and, finding that Lakeside was on the market, bought the house so that we would have an established home in this country. Then, when Clifford came to visit, he would also be near his grandparents.

"In the end this proved to be an ideal arrangement. At the time I married Piero in 1939, Clifford was four, and during the eight years before our divorce, we spent much of our time here in Keswick. You see, the second great war began in that year. Although Piero grew up in the States, he had lived much of the time in Florence, but since Italy was allied with Germany in the war, he had no wish to return there while the war continued. As a United States citizen he could have chosen to live in America, but for my sake he remained here in England."

Jane asked gently, "Was he fond of your little boy?"

Vera hesitated. "I believe he would have liked to be closer to him, but Clifford rather shied away from him. In the beginning the child resented my attention to a stranger, and subsequently I believe he was much influenced by his father. My former husband understandably held no kind feelings toward Piero and made no secret of his hostility. Then when we had no child of our own, Piero felt the disappointment keenly and perhaps resented Clifford."

Vera drew a deep breath and reached for the coffeepot to refill their cups.

"But you asked about the opera, Miss Winfield. Before I met Piero, he had already been fond of the Lake Country here in England. He disliked the heat of summer in Italy and had for several years taken a house near Grasmere for July and August, kindling his fondness for the poets of the district. He was strongly attracted by Coleridge's 'Christabel' as a subject for an opera, and when we met, he was obsessed with me as his ideal heroine. I was fair, with long red-gold hair, and he liked to talk about seeing me as his vision of the innocent Christabel, kneeling in the forest, praying for her lover. He told me my name—Vera—was like the Italian *vero,* meaning 'truth.'

"With a creative artist, it's sometimes impossible to tell how much emotion is genuine and how much simply grows out of the need to nurture the creatures of his imagination. At least, I can say for Piero that whatever triggered his initial passion for me, he came to believe his own fantasy, for he was truly devoted to me for a number of years, until a new obsession appeared. Then he left me as abruptly as if our eight marvelous years had never existed!"

Vera gave a light shrug. "In any case, to go back to the beginning, we lived together at Lakeside until my divorce was final and we were able to marry. During that period he worked feverishly on the opera, setting it aside now and then to write other things, but always returning to it with vigor. The challenge, of course, was to create an ending, and he wrangled constantly with his librettist until they achieved what he wanted."

As Vera paused, Jane asked, "Did you consider singing the title role yourself?"

"No, no, my dear, I wasn't in that league at all. Piero was distinguished enough to command the best singers and conductors of his day. Nor would it have occurred to me. I was fully occupied with making his life comfortable for him. That was enough for me.

"When the opera was finished and the time came for casting, his chief problem was finding the right mezzo to sing the part of Geraldine, the sorceress, who must be a good enough actress to appear sweetly angelic to others but to show flashes of evil to the innocent Christabel. We were in London for all the rehearsals—it opened at Covent Garden, as you know—and while I saw that Piero was wildly excited one moment and in despair the next, this never showed professionally. He was patience itself with the cast, and in the end it was an enormous success."

In answer to questions from Jane, Vera added other recollections of incidents connected with the genesis and production of the opera, ending with the remark that it was pleasant now to recall those days so long ago. "Piero was often difficult, but I could usually bring him 'round, and he came to depend upon me to keep his life in balance."

Then Jane said, "I've been rather puzzled by the circumstances of Mr. Marini's death. Have you any theory concerning his drowning?"

Vera shook her head. "I've never understood it. My son and his friends used to take the little boat out on the lake or swim from the jetty, and I often joined our houseguests there in the summer. Piero sometimes walked out on the jetty, but usually stayed well away from the water."

"Might he have got over his fear in later years?"

"I should think it very unlikely."

"Were you here in Keswick at the time, Mrs. Cox?"

"No, no. Some time after the divorce, I married Charles Cox and we lived in London. When Clifford's father died, Mr. Cox adopted him, and was very good to him always. Of course I knew of Piero's death—it was worldwide news. Clifford was grown by that time and living on his own. Actually, he was here on a visit to my parents at the time, but he would know nothing about it. He may have encountered Piero occasionally in London, but I'm afraid he was never fond of him. Clifford's somewhere about—you may ask him, if you like."

From Clifford's manner on the phone the day before, Jane doubted if she would get more than a snarl from him, and at that moment, as if on cue, the enormously fat man she had seen in the garden came into the room and spoke sharply.

"Mother, I do think this is enough. You must be tired."

"I'm not in the least tired, Clifford. Miss Winfield is a most pleasant young lady, and I've quite enjoyed our talk."

Jane decided not to push her luck. Smiling, she dropped her notebook into her bag and rose. "It was very kind of you to see me, Mrs. Cox. Thank you."

Clifford said, "I'll see you out, Miss . . . er . . ." and led the way to the door. Before he could close it behind her, Jane turned and looked into the plump, petulant face of Clifford Cox.

"Excuse me, sir, I believe I saw a lady in your garden, a Miss Geraldine Foster. Can you tell if she lives near here?"

Now the pouting expression turned to ice. "Yes, but I'm certain she does not wish to be interviewed."

And the door closed.

• 13 •

AT THE POLICE STATION IN KESWICK, JANE LEARNED THAT the record of the coroner's hearing into the death of Piero Marini twenty years ago was now on microfilm, but after some delay, she was able to get a copy. She had brought with her a photocopy of a full account of the inquest from a London newspaper, Marini's fame having drawn reporters from the London dailies to the event.

With both documents spread out on the table in her hotel room, she hoped to find something to provide background interest for her current work on Marini, and perhaps to shed further light on the curious circumstances surrounding his death.

The first witness at the coroner's hearing was the local police sergeant, who described responding to the telephone call from the Marini house asking for help.

"Who placed the call, Sergeant?"

"Miss Geraldine Foster."

"Thank you. At what time was the call placed?"

"At approximately half-past twelve—half after midnight, that is."

"What did Miss Foster tell you?"

"That Mr. Marini may have fallen into the lake, and that he was unable to swim."

"What did you do then, Sergeant?"

"I rang up the fire brigade and hopped on the engine with the lads. We arrived at the house within approximately eight minutes."

"And what did you find upon your arrival?"

"Several people were standing about in the garden and on the jetty, looking into the water. We were told the gentleman had been seen sitting on the bench at the end of the jetty and had not been seen since. The night was fairly dark, with no moon."

"And then?"

"We then took the grappling hooks from the engine and began a search of the lake bottom adjacent to the area where the gentleman might have fallen. Within a short time we located what appeared to be a heavy object."

"What was the depth of the water at that time?"

"Not much over ten feet, sir."

"Thank you. You may proceed."

"One of the lads, who is a strong swimmer, slipped off his boots and outer clothing and dived into the water. On the third try he located the body, fastened the hooks, and we were able to raise the body and place it on the end of the jetty."

"The body was that of Mr. Marini?"

"Yes, sir. He was identified by all those present."

"Was there any doubt that Mr. Marini was deceased?"

"No, sir. We attempted resuscitation, but to no avail."

"Thank you, Sergeant."

The local doctor who had issued the death certificate was followed by the pathologist from the hospital where the body had been sent for postmortem examination.

When the doctor had confirmed drowning as the cause of death, the coroner asked, "Did you find any other injuries to the body? A blow on the head, for example?"

"No, I found no marks of trauma on the body."

"Was there evidence of a heart attack or other sudden illness?"

"No. Physical signs were normal."

"We have been told that Mr. Marini was unable to swim. However, if he fell from the end of the jetty, would his body not rise automatically from the water and enable him to grasp one of the pilings of the jetty, for example? He would presumably be only a short distance from the jetty."

The doctor shook his head. "The common assumption that bodies always rise in these circumstances is inaccurate. If the person panics and inhales a quantity of water, he will begin to suffer the effects of suffocation very quickly and may continue to sink. Also, in this case, I believe the gentleman was weighted down with shoes and heavy outer clothing. However, in the event that Mr. Marini did surface momentarily, we may assume that he was in a state of panic and confusion. Even if the jetty was visible to him, he may well have been unable to reach it."

Jane laid down the copy of the transcript with a shiver, remembering her feeling of panic the evening before when she broke the surface of the lake and saw nothing but blackness around her, although it was still dusk. For Marini, the total darkness must have been overwhelming, if indeed he ever surfaced at all.

Returning to the transcript, she saw that the next person called to testify was Mrs. Emilia Marini, the widow of the deceased. Jane had been surprised to read in the newspaper account of the inquest that Tina's mother had been there at the time, having assumed the couple were living apart.

Emilia was described in the newspaper as the "beautiful, dark-haired widow of the composer, wearing a black suit and a small black hat with a filmy veil; an Italian lady who spoke with traces of her native language."

After duly expressing his condolences, the coroner asked Emilia to indicate who was present in the house on the evening of her husband's death.

"In addition to two servants, my daughter Cristina was there, and two houseguests, Miss Geraldine Foster and Mr. Edmund Traherne."

Quite a cosy little foursome, Jane thought. She'd heard of the ménage à trois. Now it seems the sophisticated "household of three" had been expanded to four.

The coroner went on, "Can you describe for us please what occurred on the evening in question?"

"Yes. I was asleep when I hear my daughter Cristina screaming. I put on a robe and run to the bottom of the stairs, where the child is standing with Miss Foster and crying out 'Babbo! Babbo!' This was her name for her father, you understand."

"Yes, quite. Were you aware at that time of Mr. Marini's absence from the house?"

"No. We occupy separate bedrooms, as my husband often works into the night and would disturb me on coming to bed."

Smiling, Jane noted that Emilia was keeping up appearances all the way. It was more likely that Marini would join Gerry Foster when he was ready to retire, while Edmund Traherne no doubt paid nocturnal visits to Emilia.

The transcript continued. "What happened next, Mrs. Marini?"

"My daughter was hysterical and unable to speak clearly, but Miss Foster say that my husband is sitting at the end of the jetty, and Tina believe he has fallen into the water. We look in the house but he is not there. Then I ask Miss Foster to call for help, and I run out through the garden."

"Did you not wonder whether Mr. Marini might have gone for a walk, thus explaining his absence?"

"No. He did not like to walk at night. He is afraid to stumble in the path."

"I see. Can you add anything further, Mrs. Marini? If not, thank you for coming, and please accept the sympathy of this court in your tragic loss."

The next witness, Miss Geraldine Foster, was described in the newspaper as a strikingly attractive lady with auburn hair, also wearing black, whose answers were given in a low voice. The lady walked slowly, as her right leg was in a cast from foot to knee.

After establishing that she had been a friend of the Marini family for the past year, the coroner asked her to describe what occurred on the night of Marini's death.

"I was sitting with Mr. Marini in his music room after Mrs. Marini and Mr. Traherne had retired for the night."

"At what time was this, Miss Foster?"

"About half-past eleven, I should think. Some time after midnight, P—that is, Mr. Marini—complained that the passage of music on which he was working would not 'go,' as he put it, and he was going out for some air. I offered to accompany him, but he said he wanted to be alone to think it out. He was often impatient when his work did not go well."

"Did you see him leave the house?"

"Yes. He walked toward the door giving on to the lake. On the wall beside the door is a rack where outdoor garments are hung, and I saw him snatch up a macintosh—an old one of mine—and put it on as he went out, slamming the door. In a moment I stepped out and noticed a cold wind had come up. Going back to the rack, I took a wool muffler and started into the garden, intending to give it to him. It was then that I saw him walking along the jetty. It was extremely dark, but I could just make out his figure as he went to the end of the jetty and sat on the bench."

"Did he often sit there, Miss Foster?"

"No, not often, because of his fear of the water. I assumed that he must be very perturbed about his music, and decided not to offer him the muffler, as he disliked being interrupted when he was working out a problem."

"Would he not have to be at the piano or at his desk to work at his music?"

"No, no. Composers hear the music in their heads, you see. He used to tell us that Mozart and Beethoven did their best work while walking in the countryside, as a reminder not to disturb him when he was thinking. He often walked alone in the daylight, but never at night."

"You did not see Mr. Marini leave the jetty?"

"No. I returned to the music room and sat down at the piano to look at the manuscript of the piano sonata on which Mr. Marini was working. I played some passages of the piece for a few minutes. Then I noticed the fire was getting low and went over to build it up. The servants had gone to bed, and sometimes Mr. Marini would let the fire go out when he worked into the night and then be furious when the room was cold. It was awkward for me to manage the logs because of my leg, but I was able to add several logs and poke up the flames."

"You have sustained an injury, Miss Foster?"

"Yes. I fell on the hillside last week and have been in a walking cast ever since."

"Please go on."

"I was putting the fire screen back in place when I looked up and saw little Tina in the doorway. She looked at me and began to scream out something about her father falling in the water. The child was terror-stricken and kept calling out 'Babbo! No, no! Babbo! Help!'

"Since I had seen him on the jetty only a few minutes before, I hurried into the garden and saw at once that he was no longer on the bench. I called his name, but there was no answer. Tina was still screaming when Mrs. Marini came down the stairs. We searched the house and garden but could not find him. That was when I called for help."

"Thank you, Miss Foster. Can you suggest what might have occurred to cause Mr. Marini to fall into the water?"

"We have all tried desperately to find an answer to that question, as you may imagine. Perhaps there was a disturbance in the water just below where he sat—a fish leaping? a floating object?—something that caused him to lean forward to investigate and accidentally tumble into the water."

"I believe the police have already put to the family and friends the question of suicide. Will you repeat for this hearing your opinion of that possibility?"

"Yes, certainly. It is quite simply out of the question. Piero lived for his music and was the last person on earth to take his own life."

"Thank you, Miss Foster. That will be all."

Next to be called was Edmund Traherne, described in the newspaper as wearing the school tie of Eton, which seemed by the standards of that day to have said it all, the old-boy network operating in full force.

"You are a friend of the Marini family, Mr. Traherne?"

"Yes. I've known Marini for a good while."

Again Jane smiled. Edmund was keeping up the time-honored Italian tradition of the *cavaliere servente,* immortalized by Lord Byron, in which the wife's lover is always publicly known as the husband's friend.

In answer to the coroner's question, Edmund said, "I must have been the last to come down. I sleep rather soundly, but I was roused by the pounding footsteps of the servants as they ran down the back stairs. My bedroom gives onto the back of the house, away from the lake, and is adjacent to the servants' staircase. I put on a robe and went to the front stairs, where I could hear voices in the garden, and went down to join the others."

"Are the servants' rooms on the same floor as your own?"

"No, no, on the floor above—in the attic."

Edmund had nothing further to add, nor did the cook and the housemaid, who declared they had heard nothing until awakened by Tina's screams.

Now the coroner asked Emilia if her daughter might appear, to which Emilia replied—rather unfeelingly, Jane thought—that the child was distraught but she saw no reason why she should not answer a few questions.

· 14 ·

THE NEWSPAPER ACCOUNT OF THE INQUEST ON PIERO Marini's death presented a touching picture of Tina, a "pretty, dark-haired child, obviously deeply distressed by the death of her father."

In the transcript of the proceedings, the coroner began, "Thank you for coming, Cristina."

"Please call me Tina."

"Yes, of course. And how old are you, Tina?"

"I am ten."

"Thank you. Now, will you tell us what you remember of the evening of Tuesday last?"

"Yes. I was in my bedroom."

"In which floor of the house is your room?"

"In the attic, in the center under the dormer window."

"Is the lake visible from your bedroom?"

"Yes. I had been asleep, but something woke me up and I couldn't get back to sleep, so I put on a robe and sat in the window seat and looked out toward the lake. It was very dark, and at first I couldn't see anything. Then I saw someone sitting on the bench at the end of the jetty. At first I didn't know who it was. . . ."

There must have been a pause, since the coroner said, "Then, did you see it was your father?"

In a whisper, "Yes."

There must have been tears at this point, since the coroner asked Tina if she was able to continue, and she said she was.

"Pretty soon I decided to go back to bed. A few

minutes later I heard a splash, and at first I didn't think anything about it. Then, I thought, could it have been Babbo? I ran to the window and he wasn't there! I ran down the back stairs and out into the garden, but he wasn't in sight, so I ran back to the house and looked in all the rooms and called him. Then I looked in the music room, but he wasn't there either, only Miss Foster. And then I thought he might have fallen into the lake!"

Again Tina must have broken down, for there were no more questions, and the newspaper described Mr. Traherne as leading the sobbing child from the room.

To no one's surprise, a verdict of accidental death was given and the hearing was closed.

Jane laid down the transcript. Why would a man so afraid of water bend over, for whatever reason, and fall into the lake? While boning up for her current assignment for the magazine, she had read the existing biographies of Marini, noting that each author had unquestioningly accepted the coroner's verdict that the death was accidental. Now she agreed with Andrew that it just didn't make sense. But could it have been murder?

Yes, there would have been time. Someone, perhaps wearing soft shoes, even bedroom slippers, could have crept along the jetty behind Marini, pushed him into the water, and slipped back into the house by a side door, before Tina went back to the window.

But why? One might say Emilia and Edmund had a motive for wishing Marini out of the way, but their lives appeared—on the surface at least—to be comfortably arranged without resorting to murder.

What about Gerry Foster? What if there had been a serious quarrel with Marini? He might have told her he wanted to break off the relationship. Jane had learned from Vera that Marini's fancy could be caught by a new love and he could ruthlessly dump the old one without warning.

From her encounter with the woman at the lake, it was clear Gerry's passion for Marini had never waned, even after twenty years. She could have done it. Her walking cast no doubt had a soft sole, which would have made no noise on the boards of the jetty. There was, after all, only her word for what occurred between them before Marini's death. Had guilt now turned her mind, so that she blocked out her own deed? Psychiatry would say it was entirely possible.

Jane thought, Am I being fanciful? Curious accidents did happen every day in the week. Did she and Andrew simply have murder on the brain?

That evening, in their London flat, Jane put that question to her husband.

Holding Laura on one knee, James pondered, adopting what Jane called his solicitor's expression. "No, love, I don't think you and Andrew are unreasonable," he said at last. "I agree the accident theory is unconvincing. If there had been an obvious suspect lurking about with a flaming motive for murder, the police might have thought so too."

The baby's sapphire-blue eyes looked at Jane with such a mirror image of James's expression that Jane broke into giggles. "Laura thinks you're right, don't you, darling?"

Jane reached for the baby and, with a kiss on the rosy cheek, set her on her feet. "Let's show Daddy how far you can walk!"

Absorbed for a time in baby rituals, they put aside thoughts of crime, past or present, but when Laura had been bathed and put down for the night, James returned to the topic.

Over their coffee he said, "I've been wondering

about Emilia and Edmund. Andrew told you that in his will, Marini left his wife Emilia the house in Florence and a modest yearly stipend, but the lake house and the remainder of the royalties on his music were left to his daughter Tina. The question is, did Emilia know about his will?"

"Yes, I see. What if she and Edmund assumed everything would go to her? It would have given them a clearer motive for shoving Marini into the lake."

"Precisely. Also, your theory about Gerry Foster is entirely possible. Even if Marini hadn't gone so far as to threaten breaking off with her, she might have suspected he was into a new relationship and decided to make sure no one else could ever have him."

Jane nodded. "By the way, darling, my having met oozy Edmund in Florence with Andrew must have done the trick, because I rang up today and have an appointment to meet with Emilia tomorrow afternoon!"

Accordingly, shortly before four o'clock the following day, Jane took a taxi to the address in Hampstead given her on the telephone by Edmund Traherne.

The handsome Georgian house stood on a hill, close to the road in front but with a generous garden at the back, as Jane saw when she was shown into a room with tall windows giving onto green lawns fringed with the reds and browns of autumn foliage. Although it had been a day of overcast skies and fitful showers, the October weather was still mild. Yet Jane saw not only a fire burning in the hearth, but felt a warmth in the room that could only come from central heating turned up to a level rarely encountered in English homes.

"My dear Miss Winfield!"

Edmund Traherne strode forward, taking Jane's

hand. "How delightful to see you!" The pouches under his eyes were already rimmed with red. Must have started early today, Jane thought.

Behind him a maid held the arm of a woman who took a few halting steps and then subsided into a wheelchair, which the maid pushed into the room.

"By the fire, please. Closer . . ." A deep, rich voice, the English markedly accented.

Then Edmund, hovering. "Are you comfortable, my love?"

"No! Move my foot, if you please."

As he knelt by the wheelchair, Edmund hissed to Jane in a stage whisper, "There is still some loss of movement on the left side, you see."

When the foot had been moved to the patient's satisfaction, Edmund rose. "Emilia, my dear, this is Miss Winfield, the young lady I met in Firenze with our little Susie."

While Edmund dispatched the maid for tea, Jane studied Tina's mother with some curiosity. At fifty-five, she was still a handsome woman, full-bodied like most Italian women her age, with huge black eyes which stared enigmatically at her.

"It's very good of you to see me, Signora Marini."

"I do not like the press, but Edmund say you are simpatica."

Flashing a grateful smile at Edmund, who gave a courtly little nod, Jane began with questions about Piero Marini's habits of composition at the time of his marriage to Emilia. Feeling some awkwardness in speaking about Marini in the presence of Emilia's lover, she soon saw this was no problem for Emilia and Edmund, who seemed to regard themselves as a conventionally married couple.

Once begun, Emilia spoke freely of the ten years of her marriage to Marini. "Piero was much much older than I—he was sixty when we met, and I was a girl of twenty." (Make that twenty-four, Jane smiled to herself, duly writing in her notebook.) "My mother is very angry when I marry a divorced man, and one so old, but Piero never seem old. It is perhaps his music that keeps him young. He is so filled with, how you say, lively . . . ?"

"Vitality?" Edmund put in.

"Yes, that is good word. Of course, sometimes he is unhappy when the music does not go well, but when it is right for him, he is like a boy—excited, happy!"

Edmund nodded. "Marvelous chap!"

"He not like to be disturbed when he was working. At first, this make me unhappy, but soon I learn it is best not to bother him. Sometimes we must live in the house at the lake, where it is so cold, even in the summer, but he work well there, and he like walking in the hills."

Jane said, "I believe your little girl was born there, was she not?"

Emilia frowned, her mouth petulant. "Yes. I have bad time—I suffer very much. At first, Piero is so tender, so loving to me. Then when I am well, he forget it all, he is so excited to be a father. He go about with the baby everywhere, so proud of her. I never see a man care so much for a bambina."

"And she was very fond of her father, was she not? I understand his death was a severe blow to the child."

Edmund nodded. "Yes, poor little Tina. She was devastated."

The maid arrived with the tea, pouring for Jane and Emilia, while Edmund patronized a tray with an array of bottles and glasses.

Jane said, "I believe you were both there at the lake when Mr. Marini died. Had you been staying there for long?"

Emilia turned to Edmund. "How long? Do you remember?"

"We came up about a week earlier, as I recall. Emilia and I had been here in London for a time. You understand, Miss Winfield, Marini was a splendid fellow, but he was not a faithful husband. After putting up with his affairs for some time, Emilia met me at a friend's home and we soon grew to care for each other. There was no chance of divorce for her because of the child. Marini would never have given her up."

"I see."

"Marini insisted on maintaining the outward appearance of domesticity until little Tina was grown. On this occasion he had Gerry Foster, his current lady, living in the house, so I came along as well. There was no longer any bitterness between Emilia and Marini, and we all got on comfortably enough."

Emilia's black eyes darted toward Jane and back to Edmund. "He make it sound so pretty, but I do not like it so well."

Casually, Jane said, "I was in Keswick the other day and saw Geraldine Foster."

Emilia's eyes sparked. "Gerry? At the lake?"

"Yes."

Edmund said, "How extraordinary! We heard she had gone off to India with some chap soon after Marini died. I had no idea she was in England. What was she doing in Keswick?"

"I believe she lives near there." Choosing her words carefully, Jane added, "I wondered what sort of person she was twenty years ago. Did she seem a bit—well, unstable or odd, in any way?"

Edmund laughed. "Not Gerry! She seemed to me a sensible young woman with her feet squarely on the ground."

Emilia pouted. "Not so young, Edmund. She was older than I, remember."

"So she was, by a few years at least."

"I do not like to see her with Piero. Whatever you say, he was still my husband."

Edmund patted Emilia's hand. "Of course, my dear."

Deciding on a long shot, Jane said, "I believe Mr. Marini's first wife, Vera, had a son, Clifford Cox."

Now Edmund smiled broadly. "Yes, good old Clifford. He's the chap who introduced us! He was a friend of yours, my dear, was he not?"

Emilia's dark eyes slid to one side. "Clifford? Yes. He is with Hawkins and Booth, the music publishers who did Piero's work in England. That is how I came to know him."

"Haven't seen him in donkey's years, have we?"

Emilia was silent.

Asking about the forthcoming production of Marini's opera, *Christabel,* Jane learned that Emilia was looking forward to the occasion but not to the presence of her daughter.

"I did not believe Cristina would come," she said, petulance twisting her mouth. "She kill her husband, and now she say she is coming to the opening."

Edmund hemmed. "Really, my dear, Tina was not at fault."

"So you say. How do I know? I was fond of Mario, and Carlo too. Like brothers, they were. Poor Carlo, he must be so unhappy."

Remembering Andrew's description of Carlo's visit to Casa Marini, Jane thought Carlo was more consumed with greed than with grief over his cousin's death, but she said nothing. Emilia seemed to ignore the fact that her daughter's husband had attacked her with a lethal weapon.

Before concluding the interview, Jane managed to slip in a few questions about the occasion of Marini's drowning in the lake, but she learned nothing beyond what the coroner's hearing had revealed. Neither Emilia nor Edmund seemed reluctant to talk about the occasion, but if there *was* any guilt, Jane reflected, they had had twenty years to polish their act.

• 15 •

IN THE MORNING AFTER TINA CAME BACK TO CASA Marini, Andrew lay in bed, his mind a turmoil of images from past and present. Tina had slipped away in the early hours of the morning, saying they must be discreet.

"We mustn't be obvious to the servants," she had whispered.

"But darling, why? We're both free—surely we can do as we like?"

"It's not quite a month since Mario died. It wouldn't look right, would it? Besides, I want to keep our secret to ourselves for a while." And with a gentle kiss, she had gone.

Now Andrew felt, along with the flood of gratitude to whatever gods there be for the fulfillment of his passion, a gnawing sense of guilt toward Norma. In his other fleeting relationships with women, no one had ever rivaled his unquestioning love for his wife. It was, in fact, the failure of any other woman to contest that affection that had turned him away from making closer ties.

Not that Norma was perfect—far from it. In the

three years of their marriage, they had sometimes quarreled and made up, but each time they learned more about each other, their tastes, their attitudes, their ways of dealing with their feelings. What he could never match in anyone else was the feeling of rightness. She was his darling, the center of his being. Whatever uncertainties each may have felt about jobs, careers, people, family, they talked to each other with the utmost freedom, sharing a mutual trust that was unshakable.

Now that he had told Tina he loved her, he couldn't avoid feeling he had betrayed Norma. Irrational, of course. After five years, no one would blame him for finding a new love.

Then, as he thought of Tina, he flamed with longing. He wanted her with him now, this moment, to caress the black silk curtain of her hair, to see the beauty of her face and body and relive the exhilaration of knowing she cared for him too.

How many hours before he would see her again? Would she come to the workroom this morning? Would he have to wait until lunchtime? Luigi came with his breakfast tray, but no sign of Tina.

Turning over his notes from the day before, he expected now to work with renewed vigor, but his mind refused to focus. Ironic that when she was gone, he had been too frantic with worry to get on with his work, yet now, as he scanned the staves of music he was currently working on, the black notes slid away into restless daydreams.

Remembering his promise to Susie, he rang up the number in Ravenna she had given him and reported that Tina was back, also calling Jane in London to give her the news.

Back at his desk, he ground out an hour's work, but by mid-morning he threw down his pen and strolled into the kitchen, finding Anna in a surly mood which gave him no comfort. Back through the deserted sitting room and out to the terrace. No Tina.

Seeing Luigi in the garden, half-heartedly sweeping up fallen leaves, he asked, *"Dov'è la signora?"* and was told she had gone out an hour or so before.

Back to the workroom, where he forced himself to get on with his notes. Surely she would be back in time for lunch, but at half-past twelve Luigi came with his tray, signaling that Tina was still away.

Now the fear that had haunted him during the days of her disappearance came surging back. What if the person who had threatened her life had simply waited for her to come back?

Last night, as they lay in bed, he had asked her what had frightened her, and she told him there had first been a letter, then two phone calls.

"What did the letter say?"

"It said, 'I am going to kill you.' "

"In English or Italian?"

"In English."

"Did you keep the letter?"

"No, of course not. I thought it was someone's idea of a joke."

"And the phone calls?"

"The first one said, 'Did you get my message?' The voice was muffled, and I knew it must mean the note, so I said, 'Yes. Who is this?' and they said, *'Morte.'* "

"Death!"

"Yes."

"Did the voice sound at all familiar?"

"No."

"And the second call?"

"That happened just before I went away. The same voice said *'Morte!* Be prepared!' "

"Darling," Andrew had whispered, "why didn't you tell me about it?"

"I don't know. At first I didn't believe it. Then I was suddenly so frightened, I just ran away."

"Where did you go?"

"I drove to Bologna, thinking I might stay there, but I wanted to get farther away, so I left my car at the station and took the train up into Switzerland. There was a place on Lake Brienz where I had gone as a child with Babbo and Mamma, and I thought I would feel safe there. It reminded me of Babbo, you see."

With a sting of tears behind his eyes, Andrew had held her close to him. "And now? What if the messages start again?"

"I don't think they will. By the end of the week I sort of came to my senses and realized it must be somebody trying to frighten me. If they really wanted to kill me, why wouldn't they just do it? Surely they wouldn't write me silly notes and make phone calls."

"Yes, I see."

"I think it was simply being there that cleared my head. It's so beautiful, and every day I walked by the lake. One day I took the cable to the top of the mountain. When I was little, it seemed scary and Babbo had to hold on to me, but the view is awesome."

"I wish I'd been there with you."

Tina had put her hand caressingly on his face. "I thought a lot about you, Andrew. That was when I decided to forget it and come home. I wanted to come back for you."

In the afternoon, Andrew went out to the terrace earlier than their usual coffee time, hoping Tina would be there, but no sign of her. For more than an hour he tried to read, paced the garden, drank three cups of coffee. Then the door from the house opened and Tina came toward him, smiling.

On his feet, he moved toward her and was met with a hand, palm out.

Her voice was low. "No, darling, we mustn't. Not yet. Luigi will be here with my coffee."

Stretching out on her chaise, she gave him a look of such glowing affection that Andrew's flash of irritation sputtered out. Dropping into his chair, he let his eyes move over her body. Would he ever lose this exultation? Like Keats's Lycius, gazing at Lamia,

> . . . his eyes had drunk her beauty up,
> Leaving no drop in the bewildering cup,
> And still the cup was full.

"You're undressing me, sir." Tina's dark eyes glimmered.

Andrew grinned. "I only wish I were. By the way, my Lady Love, where have you been all day? You might leave a message for your knight, so palely loitering."

"I had to get on with the papers for Mario's estate. I thought you would know."

"Is cousin Carlo still hanging around?"

"Yes, of course. He was furious I had gone away, but he calmed down and we managed to get through a load of work."

"Good. He came storming over here the day you left, demanding to know where you had gone."

"Oh, the beast. Luisa dropped in at the house just as we were finishing for the day. She seems to think she should get some of Mario's money on the grounds they would have married if he hadn't died first."

"That's pretty thin, I should think, unless Mario left her something in his will."

"Yes, but he didn't. If we had divorced, he would have made a new will, I suppose, but as Luisa so aptly said, he didn't know—"

Tina broke off with a shudder. "I still can't believe Mario's dead. Anyhow, Luisa is cosying up to Carlo, hoping to get a handout from him, apparently. At least she doesn't expect anything from me. Our mutual-hatred society's been going on for a long time."

"There's not much reason for you to feel benevolent toward your husband's mistress."

"Exactly. Luisa doesn't really need money, you understand, but everybody always wants more."

Andrew smiled. "I don't."

Startled, Tina studied his face for a long moment. "I really believe you don't!"

For the next few days, Andrew lived in a fevered haze of joy mingled with anxiety. During the time they spent together, he felt not only a growing love for Tina, but a fierce protectiveness, a desire to shield her from harm. While she seemed confident that the threats to her life had been merely a hoax, Andrew outwardly agreed but was haunted by fear.

After that first day of miserable uncertainty, he had persuaded her to tell him her plans for the day, so that sanity returned to his working hours, knowing that he would see her next at lunch, or coffee, or whatever. One evening they went out with Susie and Alex, who were back in town, and on several evenings Tina came to the workroom and helped with the endless photo-copying of documents, the rented machine slow but steady.

On Friday evening she announced over dinner that

the paperwork on Mario's estate was winding down and she would be free over the weekend.

"Carlo's off to make a duty visit to an aunt, so he won't be bugging me."

"Wonderful! Let's celebrate!"

"All right—but how?"

Andrew took her hand, and she made no objection, even though Luigi might appear at any moment with the next course.

"How about a few days in Venice?"

Now she did put up a warning finger, but her face was radiant as she whispered, "Yes, why not?"

The next morning they set off in Tina's Ferrari, ignoring the intermittent showers of rain that came with the early November weather. Morning gloom often gave way to afternoon glory at this season, but Andrew would scarcely have noticed a snowstorm or a heat wave, absorbed as he was in having this interlude with Tina.

Venice had seemed to him an ideal choice, for his only visit there had been in his student days, before his marriage. When he had come to Italy with Norma one summer, they had driven from Milan down to Rome and Capri, then up the coast and into France, leaving Venice for another time—a time that never came. The recollection still brought the old familiar stab of pain, and probably always would, but now Venice beckoned as a place that, for him, would belong only to Tina.

· 16 ·

VENICE IN NOVEMBER, WHILE NOT WITHOUT TOURISTS, WAS free of the crowds Andrew remembered from the summer of his university days. Leaving the car in the car park, they took the waterbus along the Grand Canal, passing the wonderfully seedy and decaying palaces that lined the canal.

At the Piazza San Marco they walked the length of the huge square, looking back at the breathtaking facade of the basilica, like an enormous cake, its Romanesque arches iced with Byzantine domes and minarets.

Andrew had booked at the Bonvecchiati, the only hotel he knew, on a small canal not far off the end of the piazza. The hotel was as attractive as he remembered, if three times the price, and their room gave a pleasant view of canals, rooftops, and church spires.

Stowing their bags in the room, they set forth, well-bundled against the wind that streaked the sky with moving shapes of black and gray.

"The cathedral first?" Andrew asked.

"Yes, good idea. It probably closes early in the off-season."

Standing in the interior of the great church, Andrew was reminded again how different was this artistry from the Gothic creations of the same period. Unlike the severe beauty of Notre Dame or Chartres, where single, high-vaulted naves were lighted only by the delicate tracery of stained glass, here the massive round arches and cupolas were encrusted with the dazzle of gold and colored mosaics, every inch from top to bottom glimmering with figures and scenes in an orgy of Byzantine splendor.

For half an hour he followed Tina up the ancient steps to the galleries that skirted the mosaic-covered walls, and down again to the marble floors that undulated alarmingly from the sinking foundations of the great building, until they were shunted out by the priests at closing time.

Outside, a misty rain wet the stones of the piazza and made spidery webs in Tina's hair as they walked toward the covered portico that framed the square. Looking in the shop windows at jewelry, lace, and glassware, they selected gifts for each other—a bracelet of chased gold for Tina, a pair of ruby liqueur glasses for Andrew.

Farther along the colonnade they came to Florian's, the café where the rich and famous had taken their coffee or aperitifs for decades at outdoor tables, to the music of an orchestra.

"I've never sat inside before." Andrew shook their wet jackets and hung them on the rack by the door. "No outdoor tables today."

Over their cappuccino they talked of plans for the next day.

Tina said, "If the weather's not too bad, we could go over to Torcello. I'd like to see the old church again."

Not really wanting to know, but unable to keep himself from asking, Andrew said, "Have you come to Venice often?"

"No, not really. A few times. Mario liked to go to the Lido for the gambling now and then."

"Okay," he said, "I asked for it." Useless to try to hide his anguish.

Tina reached across the table for his hand. "Darling, it's all right. It doesn't matter now. You're the one I want to be with."

Looking at that lovely face, the black hair crossing her forehead, he felt a high he hadn't known for years.

"Tina, I want you to be with me all the time. I want to be married to you. Never mind about children. We can try for adoption if we want to. Will you come to California and live with me and be my love?"

"Oh, Andrew—it sounds like heaven. But it's too soon. I can't think about the future yet." Eyes troubled, she looked down at the table.

"All right, darling, I won't rush you. So long as you love me, I'll wait."

"I do—you know I do."

"Then it's settled. No more problems."

Their stay in Venice was a jubilant time for Andrew. Secure in Tina's affection, he tried to ignore the threads of fear for her safety that brushed the fringes of his consciousness.

Tina had promised only two nights in Venice, making it all the better that the next day was graced with a warm sun. They took the motor launch across the lagoon to the island of Torcello, strolling along toward the ancient church with its forbiddingly stark exterior, so different from the rich splendor of San Marco. Inside, the plain form of nave and two aisles was barren, the mosaic Virgin on the wall of the apse restrained in its simplicity.

Standing with Andrew's arm around her, Tina breathed, "It's as I remembered it. Haunting, but I don't know why."

Then her mood lightened. Looking up at the rather plain-faced madonna above the altar, she smiled. "Are you going to tell me I look like that one too?"

"No, darling, only the one in San Miniato!"

Over a long and excellent lunch at Cipriani's, they ignored the past and spoke lightly of other things, Andrew describing something of his life at the university in Los Angeles, then talking of plans for the London production of Marini's *Christabel,* now less than two weeks away.

Tina had already made it clear they could not stay openly together in London, especially as the press would be lurking around. Now Andrew asked, "Will you stay with your mother and Edmund, then?"

Tina rolled her eyes. "Not bloody likely, as Liza Doolittle would say. No, I've booked at the Savoy. It's close to the theater, and I've stayed there before. And you?"

"Since I can't be with you, I'll stay at my friend's flat in Bloomsbury. He's going to be away, as usual. He's a travel guide, doing music and art tours all over the globe, so the flat is more or less a pied-à-terre for him. You can come visit me there, my love, even if you don't stay over."

Tina giggled. "We could have tea in the boudoir."

"Exactly."

"At least Mamma invited me to her party. Once she found out I was coming to London, she couldn't very well leave me out."

Emilia and Edmund were hosting a gathering at their house in Hampstead to follow the opening night at the opera house.

Andrew said, "It was decent of them to invite *me*. It must have been Edmund's doing, since I met him with Susie and Alex, when Jane was here."

"Well, dear sir, you do have some standing as a Marini scholar. Edmund's always been keen on knowing the 'in' people. When your book on Babbo comes out, he can tell people he knew you when."

"It will be great to be in London. Jane can't wait to

meet you. I'm afraid I did rather go on about you, but she and James are utterly reliable and will say nothing to anyone about us till you're ready to make the announcement."

It was late afternoon when they got back to the Piazza San Marco and sauntered the length of the nearly deserted square, the shops closed on Sunday, even the pigeons looking lackadaisical in the dusky light.

Tina said, "Let's wander," and for an hour or so they played the tourist game of getting lost among back streets and canals, crossing little arched bridges, following narrow walks at random, stopping for coffee at a café, and at last following signs back to the Piazza and the hotel, where it was time to change for the concert.

They had seen a notice of Vivaldi's music that evening at the church where the composer had been the organist in the early years of the eighteenth century, and agreed they couldn't miss it. Walking along the Grand Canal, past the Doge's Palace, past the Hotel Danieli, and over a bridge, they found the exquisite little church and heard half a dozen of Vivaldi's string concerti played by a fine ensemble.

Afterward, suffused with the incomparable baroque music, they walked slowly along, savoring the unusual warmth of the evening.

Andrew said, "Now for a gondola, darling. The ultimate romantic touch."

At the gondola stand most of the boats were covered, but they found one available and settled into the lovers' seats under the canopy, floating along the Grand Canal, then turning into the network of small canals, where voices from the houses above them rang out in the night.

Holding Tina, feeling her responding kiss, Andrew

felt again, as he had the first night when Tina came to his room at Casa Marini, that it was all right now. This was what he had waited for, this was the woman in all the world he wanted.

Half an hour later, as the boat glided back to its docking place, Tina looked up at a figure standing on the quay and whispered, "Oh, no!"

Clutching Andrew's arm as he helped her to her feet, she stared into the darkness at the receding figure, then breathed in relief.

"What is it, Tina?"

"It's all right. I just thought—"

"You thought you saw someone you knew?"

"Yes, but it wasn't."

Back at the hotel, Andrew saw that Tina was still shaken. "Tina, you *must* tell me. Who did you think you saw, and why were you afraid?"

"It's nothing, honestly. I was only being jumpy." She put her arms around his neck. "Just hold me, darling."

Whatever had caused her fear seemed to evaporate in the glow of their lovemaking, and the next morning, as they drove back to Florence, her mood was easy and cheerful until they reached the city. Then the troubled look came back to her face again.

"Look, darling, do you mind taking a taxi up to the house? When we left, I told Luigi I was dropping you at the station and I was going on to Siena to visit my cousins. We can't very well come back together, carrying bags!"

"Frankly, I don't care what Luigi thinks."

"No, of course not, but he would babble to anybody who asked about us. I'm not ready for that yet. You go on up, and I'll stall around for a few hours and come in later."

When she stopped the car near a taxi stand, he sat for a moment looking into her eyes. "Tina, if we love each other, you must trust me and tell me everything."

Her answer twisted his heart. "Trust? I haven't had much practice with that. Mamma's never really cared much about me. I thought I could trust Mario, but I was wrong. I guess I haven't trusted anyone since Babbo died."

· 17 ·

FOR THE NEXT FEW DAYS ANDREW SPENT HOURS WITH THE photocopier, finishing up the Marini documents before it was time to leave for London. When he had shipped off the last of the cartons to his home in Los Angeles, he knew that until he heard they had arrived safely, he would have the scholar's jitters that fire, flood, or act of God would wipe out the treasures before he had finished with them.

Tina was in and out of the house, still at the beck and call of the lawyers working on Mario's estate. "They keep telling me we're all through for the present, and then they think up another problem or another set of papers to be signed," she complained. "I'll be glad to get to London and let them manage without me for a while."

Still constrained to keep up appearances before the servants, Andrew was consoled with Tina's nightly visits to his room, where he decided Coleridge's famous lines said it all:

All thoughts, all passions, all delights,
Whatever stirs this mortal frame,
All are but ministers of Love
And feed his sacred flame.

His mood of euphoria lasted for five memorable days. Then his peace of mind was shattered again.

On the Saturday morning after their return from Venice, Luigi knocked and came into the workroom with a note "from the signora."

"Thank you, Luigi, that will be all."

His hands not quite steady, he opened the note.

Dear Andrew,
    I'm so sorry. I must go away again. I'll see you in London next Thursday for *Christabel*.

Tina

For the first time since he had known her, Andrew shook with fury. How could she do this? How could she tell him she loved him and not understand she could trust him with whatever was happening?

Certainly, the threats must have started again, and the panic she had felt earlier had again sent her flying to a place of refuge. But if she had confided in him, he would have gone with her, looked after her. Didn't she understand that?

The answer was no, she didn't. She had told him so, and he hadn't fully taken it in. Having himself been fortunate enough to live among people who took mutual trust for granted, he realized it was something Tina would have to learn bit by bit, if he would be patient and give her time.

If he had been distracted at the time of Tina's first

disappearance, it was nothing to the torture he felt now, when she had become so much a part of his life. After a restless night, he spent a miserable Sunday trying to read and hoping she would phone, his mind racing all the while with wild conjectures about where she might have gone,

Back to Switzerland again? Somehow, he doubted it. She had spoken of cousins in Siena, but that was too close to home. Susie had gone down to Rome for a few days and Alex was off somewhere sketching again. Could Tina have gone to Rome with Susie? But surely one of them would have told him.

Then there was his conviction that Tina knew, or at least guessed, who the person was who threatened her. In Venice, in the gondola, she thought she recognized someone. Man or woman? In the darkness it was impossible to tell. But how would anyone have known they were in Venice? Unless Luigi had overheard Andrew at the dining table and told someone what he had heard.

Should he ask Luigi? Not much use. If the old man *had* told, he'd never admit it, since Tina had given him a different story.

Who would try to follow her to Venice anyhow? Carlo or Luisa were both here in Florence, but the devoted Luigi would shut up like a clam to either of those two. Could Edmund have come over to try to see her again? As Tina's unofficial stepfather, he might have conned Luigi into an admission, but since Tina was coming to London in a few days, why not wait till then?

At last Andrew went out for his daily walk, following the road up the crest of the hill much farther than usual and taking a circuitous route back to the house, hoping physical fatigue would help him to sleep that night. It began to rain but he scarcely noticed, walking swiftly, head down, not bothering to look at the glimpses of the city below as they came intermittently into view.

Suddenly, a quarter of a mile from the house, he stopped.

"That's it!" He spoke aloud, into the rain. "I know where she is."

Of course, why hadn't he thought of it before? The last time she ran away, it was to a place she had been as a child with her father. Where else would she have memories of him if not in Keswick, by the lake? Yes, Marini had died there, but she had also known joyous times there in the security of his affection. She had told him she used the house off and on through the years, that in spite of the tragedy, it was the one place where she felt close to her father.

Back at the house he phoned Alitalia and booked a flight to London for the next morning, packed two bags—one with walking boots and casual gear for Keswick, the other with clothes for London—and told Anna in the kitchen he would miss her *cucina* while he was away. The next morning he took a taxi to the station and boarded the train to the airport in Pisa.

In London a taxi took him to Euston Station, where he deposited the larger bag in the "left luggage" and boarded the next train to Penrith, as Jane had done two weeks earlier.

During the long hours on the train, he began to have doubts. Why had he been so sure she would be in the house at the lake? She could be anywhere in the world. There must have been a dozen other places she had gone with her father, any of which might have beckoned her in her fear. How little he really knew of her life. But long years lay ahead of them to grow together, and no one was going to take that away from him.

Even if Tina wasn't there, the trip to Keswick would not be wasted. He needed to visit there anyhow, checking out the area where Marini had lived. It would also give him a chance to look over the scene of Marini's death. Jane had given him the full story on the phone of her adventures there, and had sent him copies of the newspaper account and the transcript of the coroner's inquest. He had said nothing of all this to Tina. No point in upsetting her with their suspicions of murder unless he and Jane came up with something substantial.

The trouble was, he had no heart for research, no real yen for sleuthing. If Tina wasn't there, the world for him was weary, flat, stale, and unprofitable, and he had no more heart than Hamlet had to stir himself to action.

But as he stepped off the train in the little town of Penrith, all the conviction of the night before flooded back. Too eager to wait for a bus, he took a taxi the fourteen miles or so to Keswick, learning on the way that his driver was a Keswick man, born and bred, but now living in Penrith, and could take him directly to the house if he wished.

"Everybody knows about the composer chap," the driver said. "I wonder they don't turn the house into one of those tourist places and charge admission. But there, some say as the daughter still comes to stay now and then with a party of friends."

"Yes, I believe she does," said Andrew noncommittally. "Do you know if anyone's there at the moment?"

"No, I couldn't rightly say. I haven't had call to go round that way of late."

When at last they drove through the village of Keswick and along the road that skirted the lake, Andrew swallowed hard against his swollen throat and felt his breath shorten. As the taxi bumped down the long drive toward the house, he saw with dismay that although the day was extremely cold, no smoke issued from any of the half-dozen chimneys.

He asked the driver to wait, and walked along the side of the house and down to the garden fronting the lake, half wondering if he would meet the disturbed woman, Gerry Foster, but no one was in sight. Heart thudding slowly, he climbed the steps to the veranda and knocked on the door.

Silence.

Now he pounded on the door and waited.

Nothing.

About to turn away, he heard a click and saw the handle of the door move slowly. Then the door opened and Tina stood in the doorway, her eyes jet black in her pale face.

"Oh, Andrew!"

He held her close, kissing her hair, her lips, her neck. "Tina, Tina! You're safe."

"How did you know where to find me?"

"I didn't. I just guessed. May I come in?"

She laughed shakily. "Of course. I'm so glad you're here. I've been so frightened. I was upstairs when I heard a car come down the drive, but by the time I went to the back window, I saw only the driver, and I was terrified. Then I looked out this side and saw you in the garden."

"Look, I'll tell the taxi driver to go on, shall I?"

Tina paused, then said with a radiant smile, "No! Let's go into the village. I've been cooped up here for days, and I'd love to get out. I'll just run up and get my coat!"

When the taxi dropped them in the town center, and the driver had handed Andrew his bag, Tina said, "Where are you staying?"

Tossing the bag over his shoulder, Andrew didn't hesitate. "I'm staying with you, my love, and I'm not letting you out of my sight."

They walked for a while, browsing in shop windows, then found a table in a corner of a tea shop to join in the afternoon ritual.

"Would you rather have coffee?"

Tina smiled. "No. Just being in England brings out the tea drinker in me."

Over the cups and crumpets Andrew said, "All right, Tina, tell me what happened. You were all right on Friday night. So it must have been on Saturday morning—"

"Yes." Her voice was low. "I had another phone call. Oh, Andrew, it sounds so silly. It was the same voice again, and it said, 'This time I mean it.' And then it repeated, *'Morte!'*"

"Death."

"Yes. I just panicked. I know I should have told you, but in a way, I don't believe it at all. It's too ridiculous, and since I had to come over to England for the opera anyway, I thought I'd come up here for a few days. I didn't want to drag you away from your work, and all for some silly threat that probably means nothing."

"Did you think I would get much work done as it was?"

"Oh, darling, I don't know. I couldn't think clearly. Half of me *does* believe it, that's the trouble."

"Yes, I can see that. Now, if it's only a cruel way of torturing you, who would be most likely to do that?"

"Probably Luisa. She hates me for killing Mario, as she puts it, but if she really wanted to murder me, wouldn't she just knife me and be done with it?"

"Maybe she isn't keen on spending time in prison."

"Yes. I suppose she would at least try to choose a time or place where she wouldn't be caught."

"What about cousin Carlo?"

"I've thought about that, but it doesn't seem to fit, somehow."

"What's he like? I've only seen him the one time he came to the house, demanding to know where you'd gone."

"He has a quick temper, that's true, but I don't see Carlo going in for the letters and phone calls bit. Still, he could be capable of violence, like Mario. They were very much alike in many ways. More like brothers than cousins. Mamma was crazy about both of them. Would you believe, she's invited Carlo to her party in London Thursday night?"

"Speaking of Mamma, what about Edmund?"

"It's certainly more his style, the sneaky approach. But I can't see what he would gain by frightening me, if he wants to charm me into giving him some money."

After their tea, as they waited at the taxi stand, Andrew said, "What about dinner this evening?"

Tina grinned. "There's plenty of food in the house."

"You can cook?"

"Of course. I didn't grow up around Anna for nothing!"

THE NEXT MORNING AS THEY LINGERED OVER BREAKFAST, Tina said, "We'll have to get back to London tomorrow, but what about today? You haven't been here to the Lakes before?"

"No, it's been on my list, but I've never made it."

"Then let's hire a car and I'll show you around. In the summer the traffic on the roads is horrendous, but no problem now. We'll do a literary tour, shall we?"

Andrew laughed. "I'll never find a more glamorous tour guide, that's for sure."

When the phone rang, Tina looked puzzled. "Who on earth?"

Then Andrew heard her say, "Oh, of course, Mr. Elton. The central heating is fine. Yes, I expect to leave tomorrow in the morning. Yes, if you will, please. Thank you!"

Smiling, she explained, "That was the estate agent who looks after the house for me. He wanted to be sure everything was in working order. He's marvelous. I'd never be able to keep the place without Mr. Elton."

The day was overcast, with a chill wind biting their faces whenever they left the warm cocoon of the car, but the gray skies suited the bleak landscape of leafless trees and brownish lakes, and made more haunting the forbidding crags of the fells.

"We'll start off with Dove Cottage in Grasmere," Tina announced as she drove.

"What about Coleridge? Didn't he live here in Keswick?"

"Yes, but there's no house of his to visit. The poet, Robert Southey, took him in and more or less kept him and his family off and on for years at Greta Hall, right in the heart of the village, but the hall is now a school."

In Grasmere, at Wordsworth's cottage, Tina moaned. "How on earth did they manage with all those children and endless visitors in this tiny house? Whole families used to come and stay for weeks at a time."

Andrew patted her hand. "You see, dear, Wordsworth had a devoted sister and a devoted wife both waiting on him hand and foot, lucky fellow, while he roamed the countryside looking at daffodils."

"Poor things—the women, I mean. It must have been heaven when they moved to Rydal Mount, sort of from rags to riches."

"Not as rich as dear old Ruskin, I imagine. Didn't he live around here somewhere?"

"Oh, absolutely. He's next on our list after Wordsworth."

At Rydal Mount, near Ambleside, they browsed among the Wordsworth memorabilia and wandered briefly through the now frost-nipped gardens that had been landscaped by the poet himself. Then they drove on to Lake Coniston to visit the magnificence of Brantwood, the home of the Victorian art critic, John Ruskin.

From the car park they made a dash through a shower of icy rain to the warmth of the house, moving from room to room, where the walls were dappled with drawings and watercolors and the windows offered ravishing views of the lake and the barren peaks of the fells.

Remembering his reading from earlier days, Andrew shook his head. "What an extraordinary fellow Ruskin was. All those Victorians prided themselves on eccentricity, but I'd say he was a frontrunner in that department. A radical in art criticism—for his day, at least—and a rich man who was a passionate social revolutionary. To say nothing of his penchant for young girls of tender age—unconsummated, according to his wife, who promptly went off with the painter Millais."

Tina's dark eyes smiled into his. "All right, professor. I thought I was the tour guide on this excursion!"

Andrew laughed. "It's an occupational hazard, darling. Whenever I break into a lecture, there's a good way to stop me."

And noting they were alone in the room, he cupped her face in his hands and kissed her lightly, feeling his heart bound when she pulled him closer and murmured in his ear, "Oh, Andrew, I do love you so." Tina sighed, then detached herself gently. "Windermere next?"

Retracing the road they had followed from Ambleside, Tina presently turned off to the south.

"That's enough literary pilgrimages for one day. How about lunch?"

"Sounds good to me."

As they approached the town of Windermere, she took a side road and pulled up at an inn that offered a charming view of the lake.

"You'll like this place."

A bottle of wine between them, they dawdled through a three-course meal, Andrew knowing vaguely that the food was good but finding himself in a trancelike state of euphoria, hearing a muted refrain in his head singing, "It's going to be all right—she won't disappear again—it's going to be all right. . . ."

Hurrying into the car against a chill wind that bit into his face, Andrew noticed, on the other side of the car park, a man in a dark fur cap, bent over, studying the rear tire of his car. A fur cap—good idea, Andrew thought. He might never use it in Los Angeles, but in England, with winter coming on . . .

"When we get to London, I think I'll look for a fur cap—you know, the kind the Russians wear."

"You could use one today, darling!"

With a glance at her watch, Tina turned back toward Keswick.

"There's a place I want to take you to, if the weather behaves."

Minutes later the wind died down and a late afternoon sun broke through the clouds, casting pale yellow over the leafless trees.

Andrew laughed. "Mother Nature at your service!"

"Oh, good. Let's hope it holds."

Later, as they traveled north, the road ran beside Derwentwater, the sun turning the lake white in the rare stillness of the air. Some miles before Keswick, Tina said, "Here it is—the Watendlath road," and turning sharply right, she followed the narrow lane as it climbed the side of the fell, squeezing over to allow an occasional car to pass.

"This is one of the famous spots in the Lakes: the Ashness Bridge and 'Surprise View.' In the summer it's thick with tourists, but even now, in November, there are people. The locals come here as well as the visitors."

As the road leveled, they crossed a small stone bridge spanning a classic sparkling mountain stream, while below lay the lake and the valley. The sun had dropped behind the fells across the lake, and clouds were already forming, but the air remained still.

"It's lovely," Andrew murmured. "Is this the surprise view?"

"No. That's next."

Putting the car in a lower gear, Tina drove on up the sharp rise of the road, which seemed to move away from the lake into wooded glades, suddenly giving way to a moderate incline, where a cleared area served as a car park. A handful of cars were there as Tina pulled in.

"Probably hikers," Tina said. "They park here and take off onto the fells."

A short path led to a clearing, and without warning Andrew saw they were standing on the brink of a cliff, with a vista before them that dwarfed the view from the Ashness Bridge. Below lay almost the whole of the lake, ringed with the fells. Though dusk was falling rapidly, there was still enough light to make out the tiny islands in the lake and the lights coming on in the valley where the town of Keswick lay.

Andrew put his arm around Tina. "Yes, I see. And it *is* a surprise. From the road, you don't know this is here."

They stood in silence until footsteps behind them made them turn, as a young couple approached. They exchanged "Good evenings," and Tina drew Andrew gently up another path to a higher clearing, leaving the lower spot to the newcomers.

"This is the scary one." Tina shuddered slightly as they peered over the edge of the precipice. On the other cliff trees and scrub brush would break the fall if anyone slipped over the edge, but here there was nothing but a sheer drop.

"Babbo used to bring me up here. He loved the view, but he kept me well away from the brink. Here's the rock where we used to sit."

Beside her on the flat rock, Andrew put both his arms around her. "I'll keep you safe, Tina. Please, trust me."

Her head against his body, Tina spoke softly. "There's a legend that when people died, their ashes would be thrown over this crag, and sometimes their ghosts could be seen, floating in the air where the ashes had fallen."

Andrew rocked her back and forth as if she were a child, kissing the top of her head.

"Andrew."

"Yes?"

"Tell me about California. Where will we live when we're married? Shall I cook for you, or shall we bring Anna and Luigi?"

Her voice was that of a child saying, "Tell me a story," and he replied in the slow singsong of "Once upon a time."

"We can bring them if they'll come, darling. I live in a condo with a swimming pool, and you can swim every day. You can come to the university and have lunch with me sometimes, and all my friends will meet you and say, 'That lucky dog, Andrew, how did he get such a beauty?' And, of course, my mother will be ecstatic, and my sister and her husband will dote on you, and their children will call you Auntie Tina. And we can sometimes take weekend trips to Santa Barbara or San Diego or Palm Springs. It will be lovely, darling, and you'll be safe and happy."

As he talked he felt the tension go out of Tina's body. Presently her head began to droop, reminding him of his small niece when he held her in his lap for her bedtime story. Faintly, he heard the sounds of car motors, fragments of voices, then silence.

Reluctant to break the spell, he talked on, until he felt Tina shiver and became aware that a cold wind had sprung up.

Drowsily, Tina whispered, "Go on. Tell me more."

Suddenly alert, Andrew shook her lightly. "Tina! It's dark. We must get back to the car."

"Oh, so it is."

Tina stood up and stretched, then took Andrew's hand and stumbled down the path to the lower clearing. "It does go dark quite suddenly at this time of year. I'd forgotten."

They had crossed the road and found their way to

the car when Tina groaned. "The keys—they're in my handbag. I must have left it by the rock."

"You get in the car, darling. It's getting cold. I'll bring it."

Andrew retraced his steps to the lower clearing, moving his feet carefully to avoid tripping over obstacles, and had started up the barely discernible path toward the rock where they had been sitting when he heard footsteps behind him.

"Tina?"

Silence.

Had he imagined the sounds?

A few yards more and he reached the rock. Groping in the enveloping darkness, he at last found Tina's shoulder bag and slung it over his shoulder.

Now there was no doubt. Someone was there, a darker shape, with a light patch where the face would be.

"Hello! Can I help you?"

An animal-like snarl was the only answer. Hands gripped Andrew's arms and he felt himself being propelled backward toward the edge of the precipice.

The shock left him momentarily powerless. Then his mind said, Someone's trying to shove me off this cliff, and his muscles sprang to life. Andrew twisted his body with all the force he could muster and got his right arm free. He could feel his feet moving backward from the momentum the man had acquired by the suddenness of his attack.

If he dropped to the ground, he thought, and began to roll, they might go over the edge together, not a very happy prospect. The best shot seemed to be to give the man a solid punch to the solar plexus. Andrew had never gone in for boxing, nor did his lifestyle lend itself to fistfights or other forms of violence.

But he had one advantage. He had played tennis all his life, and he was known among his cronies for his powerful serve.

One second his right arm was free. The next, his adversary lay on the ground, choking. Andrew stumbled and fell from the force of his own blow, and Tina's handbag fell with him. In a flash he snatched the handbag and ran. As he reached the bottom of the first downhill path, he tripped and pitched full length on the rocky ground, picked himself up and raced to the car park, where he flung himself into the car.

"Lock the doors and let's get out of here! Quick!"

Tina didn't wait for questions. Getting the key out of her bag on the first try, she started the motor, turned on the headlights, and swung out onto the road.

Panting, he said hoarsely, "Some maniac tried to shove me over the edge up there!"

Tina caught her breath, gave Andrew one terrified glance, and drove on. "Could you see who it was?"

"No. No idea."

But something came back to Andrew. As he fell, half onto the man who had attacked him, his hand had for a moment felt something soft and silky, in the region of the man's head. What on earth?

Of course. It was fur.

As Tina drove rapidly back to the house by the lake, Andrew said, "I think someone was following us." And he told her about the man with the fur cap outside the restaurant in Windermere.

"You couldn't recognize the person who attacked you?" Tina asked again.

"No, but he was not as tall as I am. I would guess about five feet nine or so. Strong, obviously."

Tina was silent until they drove down the lane to

the house. Then she said, "Look, Andrew, we're going to grab our things and get out of here. We can drive straight down to London and leave the car there."

Andrew had never heard her so determined, and he said simply, "Yes, all right."

On the journey to London, Andrew took over the driving when they reached the motorway, and Tina leaned back with closed eyes. They had given up speculation on the who and why of what had happened on the mountain, but Andrew was haunted by the fear that Tina had actually been the intended victim. The man may well have taken the opportunity to get him out of the way, leaving Tina unprotected.

But why did he keep saying "the man"? He didn't really *know* it was a man. It all happened so fast. A tall, strong woman, wearing slacks and a fur cap? Yes, it was possible.

• 19 •

JANE WAS ON THE PHONE IN HER LONDON FLAT. "ANDREW'S coming and bringing his Tina! Can you be home early, darling?"

"Absolutely. Tell Andrew I'll be there if I have to cut a client off in mid-sentence."

Jane put down the phone and turned to her infant daughter. "Daddy's coming home early tonight!"

Sapphire eyes solemn, Laura said carefully, "Dad-dee."

"Yes, darling, and Uncle Andrew too!"

A pause. "An—doo."

A few hours later introductions had been made,

Laura had been warmly admired over drinks, and with the arrival of the babysitter, the four had adjourned to Andrew's favorite restaurant.

Talk was easy and relaxed but very much on the surface, as Jane and James carefully avoided any allusion to Tina's flight to the house at the lake. Andrew had given Jane a quick report on the telephone, trying to make light of the threat that had driven Tina away from Florence for a second time, and making a joke of the roving maniac who had attacked him the evening before.

As they sat over their coffee, friends of the Halls stopped by their table, a fellow solicitor and his wife, who had recently returned from a holiday in Interlaken.

"It's a marvelous time to go—the summer crowds are long gone and the skiers are not yet out in full force!"

When they had moved on, Jane noticed Tina's face drooping and downcast. While Andrew and James were absorbed in conversation, Tina stared at the tablecloth, then looked up to catch Jane's compassionate gaze, a sharp flash of some indefinable emotion clouding her eyes.

Covering her brief lapse of attention, Tina said, "I was in Switzerland not long ago. At Lake Brienz. Have you been there?"

"No, never. It must be lovely."

"Yes. I used to go there as a child with my parents. There's a statue down by the lake of a young woman, and it says the statue was a gift to some poet from the women of Brienz, but when I asked people there why the women gave the statue, they didn't know. Isn't it odd?"

Jane smiled. "Maybe he was an early feminist!"

Tina shrugged. "Maybe. By the way, Jane, I saw a

copy of the piece you did after your interview with Mamma. You were clever to make it sound interesting, since Mamma's sole concern in life is her own comfort and convenience."

"It was good of her to see me."

"It must have been Edmund's doing. He was quite taken with you, I hear."

"They were kind enough to invite us to their party tomorrow evening."

"Oh, good. I phoned Mamma this afternoon, and she tells me she refuses to sit in the wheelchair. She's going to sit in a wing chair and receive the guests from there. She's so vain—as if anyone would care!"

Back in their flat, over a nightcap, James said, "Tina's a stunner, all right. So what do you think, love?"

"Beautiful! Andrew looks so happy at last. Surely the threats to Tina's life can't be serious. I couldn't bear for him to be hurt."

"So what did you two talk about *chez mesdames*?"

Jane frowned. "I *had* hoped for some girl talk in the powder room, but no luck. As we lipsticked, I said you and I both thought Andrew was a very special person, and she gave me a glowing look and said, Yes, he was, and then stood up with a sort of let's-go-back look."

"Well, darling, she doesn't really know you except as Andrew's friend. She'll warm up soon enough, if I know my dear wife."

"I hope so. I'm afraid she's still pretty worried. Once, at dinner, she had the oddest look in her eyes. It was just after the Bartletts had stopped by, chatting about Switzerland. You remember Andrew told us the first time Tina disappeared, she had gone up to Lake Brienz, and when the Bartletts mentioned Interlaken, which is not too far from there, her face fell a mile.

She covered it beautifully, but it must at least have reminded her of a time of very real fear."

By a quarter past seven the next evening, the Coliseum in St. Martin's Lane swarmed with opera-goers, the lobby a crush of people, the stairs a slow-moving mass. They were among the minority in evening dress, Jane noted, not with surprise. That ancient tradition survived at the opera only in places like Glyndebourne or for a handful of socialites at Covent Garden and elsewhere. Since some of the solicitor crowd liked to dress at parties, she had used Emilia's black-tie affair as an excuse for a new gown, a chiffon that James had assured her was smashing.

With her press tickets, they had good seats in the orchestra, and just before the lights went down, Jane quietly extracted a tiny notebook and pen from her evening bag. When reviewing, she seldom wrote extensive notes during a performance, but an occasional squiggle was often enough to remind her of a point she might otherwise forget.

When the lights were lowered, a Distinguished Person from the support group of the English National Opera came on stage, announcing the presentation of a plaque to the widow of the composer. Emilia, resplendent in black satin, took a few steps out from the wings, graciously expressed her thanks, and retreated to enthusiastic applause. No mention of the composer's daughter.

With the arrival of the conductor in the pit, the audience rose for the playing of "God Save the Queen," Jane smiling at the tune so familiar to American ears, ironically celebrating independence from the mother country.

The orchestral prelude to the opera began with the music of the lament, its stirring chords foreshadowing the time when Christabel is believed to be dead. The music then shifted to the eerie sounds introducing the first scene, late at night in the forest.

Marini had composed the opera in two acts, each with three scenes, and as the curtain rose, Jane noted the excellent set, with the battlements of the castle hanging in a misty backdrop, as Christabel knelt downstage by the oak tree, praying for her lover, the soprano managing to look and sound innocent without being saccharine.

When the lady Geraldine appeared, the orchestra gave the theme Marini had ingeniously devised for the sorceress, a melody of exquisite tenderness, with a twist of dissonance in the harmony that disturbed without being obtrusive. The listener was made to feel that something was wrong here, a touch of evil beneath the surface.

In the following scene, in Christabel's bedchamber, the ominous undertone was heard again, as the flash of Geraldine's evil eye was first revealed to Christabel —and to the audience. The mezzo singing Geraldine handled this superbly, her voice dropping to a hoarse croak and instantly reverting to gentle sweetness.

Scene three, in the baronial hall, featured the fine baritone who was singing the role of Sir Leoline, Christabel's father, as he became enamored with the beautiful Geraldine. Then Bard Bracy, the basso, sang the story of his dream of a bright green snake coiled around an innocent dove, but Papa misread the symbolism, assuming Geraldine was the innocent dove, and promised to crush the snake.

In the climactic moment before the first-act curtain, Christabel fell at her father's feet and begged him to send the woman away, but this cut no ice with the infatuated Sir Leolinc, who spurned his daughter and walked off with his new lady love.

At the interval, Jane and James worked their way up the stairs to the bar on the dress circle level, where Andrew had reserved a table and a bottle of champagne.

Tina, looking dazzling in a black gown, glowed as James said, "Your father's music is superb!"

Over their champagne they agreed on the excellence of the production, hearing similar expressions of pleasure from people around them. As one man passed their table, they heard him say, "Marini's music is so *accessible,*" and a woman's voice, "Thank heaven for that!"

Andrew grinned. "Only in our century would anyone have used that word, 'accessible.' It never occurred to musicians from Bach to Brahms to write music people didn't actually want to listen to. In this century we're grateful to composers like Richard Strauss and Prokofiev and Piero Marini for music that appeals to a sophisticated audience but doesn't offend the ear."

Tina nodded. "I remember hearing Babbo say the atonalists were going up a blind alley. I must have been eight or nine, and I had this picture of some men walking into a cul-de-sac, with high walls on either side. It was years before I knew what he meant!"

Laughing, Andrew said, "Not a bad analogy, anyhow."

After the interval the final act of the opera more than matched the success of the first, which had ended precisely where Coleridge's poem broke off. Now Geraldine cast her spell on Christabel, who was saved by the kiss of her lover, the powerful music of the lament giving way to the triumphant love duet which ended the opera.

"No problem with this review," Jane murmured to

James as they made their way out. "It'll be a pleasure to write."

And collecting Andrew and Tina, they found their Volvo and drove to Hampstead.

• 20 •

ALTHOUGH THEIR FOURSOME WERE AMONG THE EARLY AR-
rivals at the party in Hampstead, Emilia Marini was already established in her wing chair in the large reception room, Edmund Traherne standing at her side. According to Tina, they had arranged to take Emilia in her wheelchair out of the opera house the moment the curtain went down, so she and Edmund could be ready for their guests.

As they joined the receiving line, Jane was prepared for a certain lack of warmth between Tina and her mother, but not for the icy antagonism she saw. Emilia's black eyes were expressionless as she held out a languid hand. "Cristina."

"Hello, Mamma." Not even a perfunctory kiss. "I believe you've met Miss Winfield. This is her husband, James Hall, and Professor Andrew Quentin."

A curt nod from Emilia, who still stared at Tina. "So you disposed of Mario, I see."

"Mamma! He tried to kill me!"

"So you say. Carlo seems to believe your story. Such dear boys, both of them——"

Edmund, who had been occupied with the preceding guests, turned in time to put out his arms to Tina. "My dear, dear girl—how lovely you look." As he

133

embraced her he whispered something in her ear, at which they both laughed, and as other guests pressed behind, Edmund oozed cordiality at Jane and Andrew and expressed his delight at meeting the husband of "the lovely Miss Jane."

The room filled steadily with new arrivals, soon reaching that stage of genteel overcrowding that made for the best kind of party, where mingling and regrouping were made easy. Waiters circulated with champagne, while in an adjoining room, a long table was laid with delicacies.

Tina was soon claimed by admirers and people eager to meet the composer's daughter, Andrew was drawn into a corner by a fellow Marini scholar, and Jane and James encountered various acquaintances, from music critics to people from the solicitor crowd. Tina's remark that Edmund knew everybody was soon evident. In addition to the cast and other luminaries from tonight's opera, famous faces turned up here and there from the world of music and theater, from the society columns, even from the political corridors of power.

As Jane chatted amiably with a violinist she admired, she heard her name called and saw a couple approach: an attractive man with neatly trimmed black hair and beard, and a good-looking young woman, her short blond hair fashionably blown.

"Susie! Alex! I didn't know you for a moment."

Exchanging kisses, Susie laughed. "Can you believe Alex in full penguin?"

"You look marvelous, Alex."

Kissing Jane's hand, Alex nodded. "You are right. I am very handsome, eh? And how you like Susie without the running shoes?"

"Dazzling!"

"Save that one for Tina." Susie smiled, looking

across the room at her friend, the center of a mostly male circle.

Seeing James not far away, Jane said, "You must meet my husband," and managed to extricate James and present him.

Then, as James and Alex were drawn into another group, Susie said, "Your James is a dream! Does he have a brother?"

Jane giggled. "No, no siblings, I'm afraid. He's one of a kind."

"You can say that again."

"But Susie, Alex is charming, and I must say he looks dashing tonight."

"Oh, he's charming all right. I'm crazy about him at the moment. But would I marry a Greek? Would I put my head in a noose?"

"But I thought he loved women's lib?"

"Listen, Jane, that's all very well for playtime, but the day we married, believe me, it would be back to macho city."

"So, you would like to marry again some day?"

Susie looked thoughtful. "Yes, I think I would. It's not too late to have a child. I'm only thirty. My first marriage was not a roaring success, but I have to admit it was more my fault than his. I married on the rebound, to coin a phrase, and that's never a good scenario."

"You were in love with someone else?"

"Yes. Mario and I had been together for several months—"

"Mario? Tina's husband?"

"Yes. I was pretty serious, and I thought he was too, until Tina showed up and it was exit Mario."

"But you and Tina are still friends . . ."

Susie shrugged. "Oh, it wasn't her fault, really. She didn't know how I felt. She was gone when I started seeing Mario, so I hadn't really had a chance to tell her much, and when she got back to Florence, Mario just took one look and it was all over. I blamed him, not Tina, if you see what I mean."

"Yes, I think I do."

"Then I married Brecht, probably because he was the first one who asked me. We lived in the States, and it lasted for a couple of years. Then, after the divorce, I went back to Italy, and by that time the thing with Mario was water under the bridge and we were all good friends."

At the grand piano against the wall behind them, someone began to play a theme from *Christabel,* and voices dropped to a hush as the soprano and tenor sang a reprise of the love duet from the opera. At the applause, Andrew and Tina came toward them, as James and Alex rejoined the circle. Their animated chatter was interrupted again by the piano, this time with a passage that Jane felt was familiar but that she couldn't for the moment place.

Then she saw Andrew and Tina exchange a smile, as a soft, unprofessional voice began to sing:

"Do you ask what the birds say? The sparrow,
   the dove?
The linnet and thrush say, I love and I love."

Of course, Marini's unpublished song. Andrew had played it for her in the workroom at Casa Marini. But who else would know it?

Turning to face the piano, Jane felt a jolt. Through a few intervening heads, she saw that the auburn-haired woman at the piano was Geraldine Foster, and by her side stood the hugely fat figure of Clifford Cox.

As the song continued and it was evident that this

was not a performance but merely a private amusement, conversations were resumed and the noise level rose to its normal genteel pitch. People drifted away from the piano, leaving a clearer view to Jane and her friends, and it was then she saw Tina's face, contorted with venom as she stared at Gerry Foster. Andrew had told her how Tina as a child had resented her father's mistress, and Jane saw that time had done nothing to change her feeling.

Now Tina moved slowly toward the piano, as if pulled by an invisible cord, drawing the rest of them with her. At the final strains of the song, Gerry Foster looked up with a smile at Clifford Cox, then at the circle of faces, none of whom she seemed to recognize.

Tina said, "Hello, Gerry."

Gerry smiled graciously. "I'm so sorry. I don't believe—"

"I'm Tina."

Gerry's eyes studied Tina's face. Then she rose and put out her arms. "Tina, my dear child!"

Tina allowed herself to be embraced, without responding, and Gerry dropped her arms. "Your Mamma didn't tell me you were coming."

"No."

Clifford Cox now broke the awkward silence with perfunctory introductions, pausing as he came to Jane. "Were you not in Keswick visiting my mother, Miss, er . . ."

"Miss Winfield, yes."

Jane wondered when Gerry Foster would make the connection. It hadn't been that dark at the lake when Gerry assaulted her, but not a glimmer of recognition crossed Gerry's face as she held out her hand with a pleasant smile.

Without another word, Tina took Andrew's arm

and walked away, followed by Susie and Alex, who covered Tina's rudeness with polite good-byes. A friend of James's arrived at their side just as a woman exclaimed, "Clifford! It's been ages!" and their groups moved gracefully apart.

Behind her, someone greeted Gerry Foster, who must have turned away, for Jane heard the lowered voice of the woman who had spoken to Clifford. "My dear, Gerry was there when he died, was she not? A dreadful tragedy. How on earth did it happen?"

And Clifford's voice, "We don't really know. It was dark. He must have fallen into the water. Poor Gerry. He was wearing her own mac, an old polka-dotted thing. It was thick with mud when they brought him up."

"How frightful for her."

"Yes, it was."

And the woman, probing, "And Clifford, darling, were you there too?"

A pause. "Actually, I was in town visiting my grandparents, but not at the lake, of course. Everyone in the village was shocked at the tragedy. How young we all were—twenty years ago. I was thirty-four, and Gerry must have been nearly forty. I was dreadfully smitten with Gerry, but she regarded me as a mere child."

Gerry must have rejoined the conversation, as Jane heard her amused voice. "You *were* a child, my dear. You still are!"

"I feel old as Methuselah. Ah, well, it was all so long ago, but one doesn't forget."

"Shall we go to the buffet?"

The three moved away, and Jane returned her attention to James and his friend.

Later, as they joined Andrew and Tina at the buffet,

Jane noticed a dark-haired man and a plump woman staring at Tina from across the room, and she heard Tina say to Andrew, "Would you believe Luisa is here with Carlo?"

When the four had settled with their food and champagne in a small adjoining room, Tina muttered, "Mamma told me she had invited Mario's cousin this evening and told him to bring a guest if he liked, but I hardly expected Carlo to bring Luisa. I should have guessed. It's just the sort of thing they would do to irritate me."

Andrew added, "Luisa made rather a scene after Mario died, blaming Tina for what happened."

The conversation turned to more cheerful topics, everyone avoiding like the plague any reference to Tina's distress at meeting Gerry Foster.

• 21 •

SUSIE AND ALEX, ON THEIR WAY TO THE BUFFET TABLE, were waylaid by a lady bristling with diamonds, an English client of Susie's who had bought several of Alex's paintings. Delighted to meet the artist himself, the woman had drawn them into her circle when Susie felt a tap on her arm and saw Carlo Renzi, his dark eyes feverish.

"I must speak to you, Susie."

Waving a vague apology, Susie moved away. "Yes, Carlo, what is it?"

"We know each other a very long time, yes?"

"Yes."

"Since the days when you are with Mario?"

"Of course. But why—"

"We are good friends?"

"I suppose so. . . ."

"Tina tells you everything about her life, yes?"

"Well, no, not really."

Carlo's darkly handsome face drew into a scowl. "But you know about the *professore,* Signor Quentin?"

"They are friends, yes."

"They are here together tonight. Is she in love with him?"

"Good heavens, Carlo, I don't know. Why do you ask?"

"She is my cousin."

"Mario's cousin."

"In Italy, as you know, it is same thing. I must look after her."

"Why don't you ask *her,* then?"

Carlo's voice shook. "I do ask her, and she say no, but I believe she lies."

Susie frowned. "I really can't help you, Carlo. Tina can surely do as she likes without consulting you. What if she does care for Andrew? What harm can it do to the family?"

With a lightning change of mood, all the anxiety left Carlo's face. "But of course, Susie, you are right. I make the—how you say?—mountain of the anthill?"

Susie smiled. "So, whose idea was it to bring Luisa tonight?"

"Luisa ask me if she can come, and Mama Emilia say, why not?"

"A nice little dig at Tina. Oh, well, no harm done, I suppose."

And with a *"Ciao,* Carlo," she retrieved Alex and led the way to the buffet.

The small room where Tina and her friends had gathered was not far from the spot where Emilia Marini sat in her wing chair, Edmund Traherne at her side, chatting with their guests. As Susie and Alex passed with their loaded plates to join the others, Emilia put out a hand to summon Susie to her side.

"Susan!" she hissed. "You know who is Gerry Foster, yes?"

"Oh, yes!"

"I am displeased she come here tonight. Is not proper."

"Did she come with Mr. Cox?"

"Yes. He ask Edmund, and of course he say it is all right. You know him, Susan. He never say no to anyone, yes?"

Susie nodded. Long years of experience with Emilia had taught her never to disagree.

"When Piero is alive, I must pretend to be polite to Gerry. But surely not now!"

Susie made murmuring noises of assent, and presently moved away to join the group in the study.

Susie put Emilia and her mutterings out of her mind, but she did wonder about her encounter with Carlo Renzi. For one thing, she didn't know how much Jane and her husband knew of Andrew and Tina. More important, she didn't know herself at this point what Tina's feelings were for Andrew. Tina had been strangely reticent about the whole thing. One day, Susie had said it was obvious Andrew was in love and asked Tina point-blank if she felt the same, only to get an evasive look and some absurd remark that it was too soon after Mario's death. Wanting to say,

"Come off it, Tina," she had refrained, seeing the troubled look on Tina's face.

Now, seeing them together away from the public gaze, Susie decided there was no longer any doubt. Tina's soft looks and Andrew's adoring glances said it all. Carlo and the Renzi family would have to learn to accept an American professor as Tina's suitor, whether they liked it or not.

It was after midnight, the party in full swing, when their group straggled back into the large reception rooms to mingle with the other guests. Andrew and Tina were the last to leave the small room, and Andrew, finding them alone for a precious moment, pulled her into his arms and held her in a heart-stopping kiss, murmuring words of affection and hearing her say, "Oh, Andrew, I do love you."

Smiling, they went out, passing Emilia's chair, where Edmund detached himself from the group surrounding Emilia and took Tina's arm. "I must speak to you, dear girl."

Andrew tactfully moved away, but in minutes Tina was back, her face flushed with anger. "Edmund's begging again. You'd think he would have the decency to avoid the subject at the party, but no!"

As a waiter offered a tray, Tina put down her empty glass and took another champagne.

"I told him they would just have to cut back on their spending, and they could start by not having bashes like this one! He's furious with me, but I don't care."

In the next half hour, they were drawn apart into various circles, when Andrew, turning to look for Tina, saw her sway and steady herself against a table.

"Darling, what is it?"

Her face was ashen. "I don't know. I must have had too much champagne. I feel so faint."

He took the empty glass from her hand and set it down. Supporting her with his arm, he took her back into the small room where they had sat earlier and led her to a sofa against the wall in a recessed alcove.

"Lie down here, dearest." Seeing an afghan over the back of a chair, he covered her gently and sat on the floor by her side. He saw her eyes close and her body relax. Then she turned onto her stomach, whispering, "I'm all right, really. I just feel terribly sleepy."

Soon her regular breathing told him she was indeed asleep. Finding the switch, he turned off the light and went out, standing near the doorway of the room to prevent anyone from disturbing her.

The champagne had been flowing pretty freely, Andrew thought. It would be easy enough to take the classic one-too-many.

From time to time he stepped into the room and peered into the darkness of the alcove where Tina slept. By one o'clock guests were beginning to take their leave. Susie and Alex came to say good night, with a smile at Tina's overindulgence.

When Jane and James came to check again on Tina's condition, Andrew said, "I'll wake her now. It's time we were going."

As he approached Tina he was surprised to see a door standing ajar in the paneled wall beyond the sofa, giving a glimpse of a corridor beyond—a door he hadn't known was there.

Bending over Tina, he put his hand gently on her back. "Darling, can you wake up now?"

Something wet and sticky covered his hand, and he called out sharply, "James! Switch on the light!"

Even before he saw the red on his hand, he could smell the blood, and he fell on his knees beside Tina, his chest rocking with pain.

Turning her head, he put his face against hers and

heard the thin sounds of air coming from her parted lips.

"She's breathing!" he shouted. "Get help! Call an ambulance!"

• 22 •

AT HALF-PAST EIGHT THE NEXT MORNING, DETECTIVE SUperintendent Fielding of the Metropolitan CID, accompanied by his cohort, Detective Sergeant Watkins, arrived at the Traherne residence in Hampstead. According to the usual practice at the Yard, the superintendent would have remained at his desk, coordinating the reports of the field work done by his subordinates, but there were times, like this one, when Fielding couldn't resist the desire to see for himself the scene of the crime and some of the key witnesses.

In the drawing room of the Traherne house, the officers found a bleary-eyed Edmund clutching a cup of coffee with trembling hands.

"Sorry to call so early, sir," Fielding said, when the introductions had been made, "but we must get on with the case as quickly as possible."

"Yes, yes, of course. Coffee, Superintendent? Sergeant? Please . . ." Edmund gestured for the men to help themselves from the tray. "Mrs. Renzi's mother and I are most dreadfully upset. We have been in touch with the hospital, but we have no definite assurance as to Cristina's recovery. Now, how can I help you?"

Fielding looked at his notebook. "I have the report

of the officer who visited the scene last evening—or I should say, early this morning. I should like now to have your account of the occurrence."

"Yes, certainly. The problem is, we have no idea what happened. Tina was circulating among the guests at the party when I saw her last."

"At what time was that, please, Mr. Traherne?"

"It's difficult to say, but I should think it was some time after midnight. I had a few brief words with her. Then some of the guests began to take their leave, and Signora Marini and I were much occupied with farewell chats—you know the sort of thing. I don't remember seeing Tina again. It must have been well after one o'clock when we heard the American professor, Dr. Quentin, calling for help."

Fielding rose to his feet. "Can you show us where this took place, please?"

"Yes, of course."

Edmund led them across the room to the small study, where whitish dust testified to the work of the fingerprint officer the night before. Indicating the sofa, with its ugly brown stains marking the place where Tina had lain, Edmund shuddered. "She was covered with an afghan. I believe the officer took it away."

Fielding nodded. "Yes. I saw it this morning. Now, sir, where were you and, er, Mrs. Marini at this time?" He had almost said "your wife" but remembered his briefing on the relationship between Edmund and Emilia.

Edmund stepped out of the study and walked toward the wing chair twenty feet or so away. "Just here."

"I see. One moment, please."

The superintendent went back into the study, walked past the sofa in the alcove, and opened the door in the paneled wall on the far side of the room, emerging into a corridor. A few yards to his right was another door, which he opened and stepped through, finding himself face to face with Edmund and the sergeant, a few yards away.

"Now, sir, did either you or Mrs. Marini leave this spot at any time during the evening?"

The implications of the question were too clear to be missed. Edmund tried waffling. "I'm not sure that I recall, Superintendent."

Fielding eyed him levelly. "I suspect some of the guests will remember."

Edmund, swallowing hard, led the way back to the coffee tray and refilled his cup.

At a stir in the doorway, they saw Emilia in her wheelchair, being pushed toward them by a maid. Clad in a deep red velvet dressing gown, her black hair pulled back in a twist, Emilia looked pale but very much in control. Dismissing the maid, she looked directly at Fielding. "I believe you wish to speak with me?"

Edmund sputtered, "My dear, I'm sure you needn't come just now—"

Ignoring him, Emilia went on. "You will excuse I am not dressed. I am an invalid, you understand?"

"Yes. Thank you, Mrs. Marini. I was just asking Mr. Traherne if either of you left the chairs where you were sitting at any time during the course of the evening."

Emilia glanced at Edmund. "And what do you say?"

Edmund flushed. "Only that I was not sure . . ."

"I see. You have forgotten, yes? You help me to what you call the W.C."

"Yes, of course. So I did."

Fielding refrained from looking at Sergeant Watkins. "Will you show me, please, Mr. Traherne?"

"Certainly." And Edmund led the way into the corridor that gave onto the paneled door in the study. A few feet farther along he opened a door into a room with floral wallpaper and a dressing table, beyond which was a toilet behind a dividing wall. "We use this as the ladies' cloakroom when we have guests."

"And did you accompany Mrs. Marini into the room, sir?"

Edmund gave a wan smile. "No, there were likely to be other ladies present. She assured me she would send for the maid when she was ready to return."

Rejoining Emilia, they took seats near the coffee tray and refilled their cups, Edmund handing a cup to Emilia.

"Mrs. Marini, approximately how long were you absent from the wing chair where you sat during most of the evening party?"

"Only a few minutes. I cannot say how long."

The superintendent looked down at his notes. "Thank you. What can you tell me about Dr. Andrew Quentin? I believe he is the fiancé of Mrs. Renzi."

Emilia's black eyes snapped. "While we wait for the ambulance to come for Cristina, the professor tells us they are planning to be married, but I know nothing of it."

Edmund interposed. "Dr. Quentin is a fine gentleman, a distinguished scholar. He explained to us that Tina was not yet ready to make a formal announcement."

"I see. Now, Mr. Traherne, will you show us please the cabinet containing the knife used in the stabbing?"

Again Edmund shuddered, but rose promptly and

led the way to a fine rosewood table with a glass top, through which were visible three gold-framed miniatures and a Florentine box in tooled leather.

"The knife was just here. I had bought it recently in Italy."

Fielding lifted the hinged top of the table. "Isn't this kept locked, sir?"

"I expect it ought to be, but I've misplaced the key and never got 'round to having another made. The things here are not exceptionally valuable, in any case."

The superintendent shrugged. They looked valuable to him, but perhaps for people with this kind of money they were only baubles.

"Then it appears that any of the guests would have access to the weapon?"

"Yes, I'm afraid so, Superintendent. Of course, one doesn't anticipate this sort of thing, does one?"

As they drove down Hampstead high street, Superintendent Fielding consulted the list of names and addresses given him by the officer who had been called to the scene in the early morning hours. "Not many people present who were personally acquainted with the young woman. The professor is staying at a flat in Bloomsbury. We'll stop there, Sergeant, and then I'll go back to the Yard and let you carry on."

"Is he expecting us, sir?"

"Yes, he was told we would call sometime this morning."

At his friend's flat Andrew admitted the officers and offered coffee.

Noting Andrew's haggard face, the superintendent repressed an impulse toward compassion. It was too early to eliminate anyone yet.

"If you will, Dr. Quentin, please describe to us what took place last evening."

"Yes. Tina—Mrs. Renzi—seemed quite well and in good spirits until I saw her almost stumble and lean against a table for support."

"At what time was this, sir?"

"It's hard to say, but I think it must have been well after midnight."

"Thank you. Please go on."

"I asked her if she was all right, and she said she felt strange. I put my arm around her, and she sort of laughed and said she must have had too much champagne. I helped her into the small room where we had taken our supper, and put her on the sofa in the alcove. She fell asleep very quickly, so I believe she was right about the champagne.

"Then I covered her with an afghan and turned out the light. After that, I stood near the door, chatting with people but remaining where I thought I could prevent anyone from disturbing her. You see, I didn't know there was another door on the far side of the room. It was in a paneled wall and wasn't clearly visible."

"And at what time did you discover what had happened?"

Andrew's voice wavered. "It must have been after one o'clock. People were leaving, and our friends the Halls were ready to go. I tried to wake her. It was when I put my hand on her back—it came away sticky, and I realized it was blood. I called to James Hall to switch on the light, and that's when I knew something was terribly wrong. Tina was unconscious, and blood had seeped down her side and soaked into her clothes and onto the sofa."

Fielding gave Andrew a moment to collect himself,

then asked, "Have you any idea who might have done this?"

Andrew shook his head. "No, not at all. But I must tell you that for some time Mrs. Renzi has been receiving threats to her life."

The sergeant wrote rapidly as Andrew recounted the details of the letter and the phone calls Tina had described. "Half the time, she was convinced they were either a joke or done by someone trying to frighten her. At other times she was seriously alarmed. Now, of course, I have to believe they were real. But as to who, or why, I simply don't know." He also recounted to the officer the attack upon them at Keswick.

"Who would benefit from her death?"

Andrew reviewed briefly the financial benefits that might accrue to Edmund Traherne and Emilia, and to her husband's cousin Carlo, as well as the motive of revenge that Luisa Valle might have. "But it's truly difficult to believe any of these people would resort to murder."

Fielding made no comment, turning instead to another topic. "How long have you known Mrs. Renzi?"

"Only since I came to Florence in late September."

"And you are engaged to be married?"

Fielding saw Andrew's sensitive face light up. "Yes!" Then, as quickly, the haunted look returned. "I have rung up the hospital, but she is not allowed to have visitors and they will tell me nothing. You have no doubt handled other cases of this kind, Superintendent. Can you give me any idea what—" Andrew's voice broke.

"What are her chances for survival?"

"Yes."

Now Fielding permitted himself a note of gentleness. "I wish I could say, but each case is different, I'm afraid. It may be a good sign that she has made it thus far."

Fielding told the driver to drop Sergeant Watkins at the Waldorf, where he would find Mrs. Susan Brecht and Mr. Alexander Spyros awaiting him.

"See you at the Yard when you've done the list."

Susie asked the sergeant to come up to their room, and greeted him with a worried frown. "Have you any news of Mrs. Renzi?"

"I'm afraid not, madam."

"Mr. Traherne has promised to ring as soon as he learns anything about her condition. Now, how can we help?"

"If you will please describe what you saw or heard last evening at the party in Hampstead?"

"That's the problem. We didn't see or hear anything relating to the attack on Tina. When we left the party, she was asleep on the sofa. She had had too much champagne and must have passed out."

"And you, Mr. Spyros? Have you anything to add?"

Alex was sprawled in a deep chair, hairy legs protruding from a voluminous robe, his face sullen. "I know nothing. If I did, I would not tell. The fuzz are pigs."

Susie rolled her eyes at the sergeant, who appeared to take no notice of Alex's remark.

"Now, Mrs. Brecht, can you suggest anyone who might have a motive for wishing to kill Mrs. Renzi?"

"Well, her mother's companion, Edmund Traherne, has lost some money recently and wanted Tina to bail him out, and she refused. If she dies, her father's royalties go to her mother, as well as some property, and so on. But I can't see Edmund actually plunging a knife into anyone. There's Carlo Renzi, her husband's cousin. A good deal of the family property would revert to him if something happened to Tina. Then there's Luisa." And Susie described the day Luisa had come to Casa Marini, cursing Tina for causing Mario's death.

Sergeant Watkins turned a page in his notebook. "Did either of you have occasion to look at a glass-topped curio table in the drawing room of the Traherne house?"

Susie looked blank. "No, *I* didn't, did you, Alex?"

At a surly growl from Alex, Sergeant Watkins said smoothly, "I should like to take your fingerprints before I leave, if I may, so that we may eliminate you from possible suspicion."

"Of course," said Susie.

"And you, sir?"

Alex said nothing for a moment. Then he grunted, "I see the table with the glass top. I recognize a knife Mr. Traherne have with him one day in Florence."

Susie said, "Oh, I remember. The one with the jeweled handle?"

"Yes. So I lift the lid of the table and pick up the knife and look at it."

The sergeant spoke softly. "And then?"

"Then I put it back in the table. What you think? You think I stab Tina with it?"

In the silence that fell, Susie caught her breath. "Sergeant, was that the knife . . . ?"

"The weapon found does answer that description, yes."

· 23 ·

AT THE HOTEL RUSSELL, SERGEANT WATKINS INQUIRED for Mr. Renzi and was received by Carlo, in slacks and a pullover, his darkly handsome face glowering.

"You are from the police. Please, you must have influence at the hospital where Mrs. Renzi was taken. They will not let me see her! I am her cousin, the head of the Renzi family—"

"I'm sorry, Mr. Renzi, I'm afraid we have nothing to do with hospital policy."

"At least she is still alive. They do tell me that much!"

"Yes, that is good news indeed. Now, if you are willing to answer a few questions, please?"

"Yes, yes, whatever you wish."

When asked to describe what he had seen and heard the evening before, Carlo declared that he had seen very little of Tina at the party, since she had been with a group of friends and he had come with Signora Valle, a friend from Florence.

"At what time did you and Mrs. Valle leave, Mr. Renzi?"

"Time? I do not know, but many guests were still there."

"Half-past twelve? Earlier, later?"

"Yes, perhaps half-past twelve."

"Are you acquainted with Dr. Andrew Quentin, Mrs. Renzi's fiancé?"

"I have met the professor, yes. But what you say is not true. She is not engaged to marry that man."

"Why do you say that, sir?"

"She does not care for him! They may have the—what you call?—flirtation, but nothing more."

"I see. Now, where may I find Mrs. Valle?"

"She is here in the hotel. Do you wish that I ask her to come here?"

"Yes, if you will, please."

Carlo dialed a number, spoke briefly in Italian, and at a tap at the door, admitted Luisa Valle.

"Luisa, this is English policeman. He wish to ask you about last night."

Wearing black stretch pants and a low-necked blouse that emphasized her ample curves, Luisa gave the sergeant a slightly hostile look and sank into a chair. Her voice just short of insolent, she said, "I know nothing of what happen to Tina, but whoever stab her is okay with me."

Plump but sexy, was the sergeant's private assessment, and a nasty piece of goods to boot.

Unruffled, he asked, "At what time did you arrive at the party, Mrs. Valle?"

"Arrive?" Luisa looked at Carlo, who shrugged. "The opera finish at soon after ten o'clock. Is not long work, you understand. We wait for a taxi and come to Emilia's place in Hampstead by eleven o'clock, *é vero?*"

Again she looked at Carlo, who said, "Yes, eleven o'clock, no doubt."

"And during the party, Mrs. Valle, did you see Mrs. Renzi?"

"Yes, but we do not speak. We are not good friends, you understand. She kill her husband, Mario, who was my lover."

"So I understand. In self-defense, I believe?"

"That is what *she* say. How do I know?"

"At what time did you leave the party?"

"Ah, that I do not know."

"Did you come in a taxi?"

"No. Some people at the party offer to drop us here at the hotel."

"Their names?"

"I do not know. A man and woman, perhaps forty years of age."

The sergeant turned to Carlo, who shook his head. "They tell us their names but I forget."

"At what time did you arrive here at the hotel?"

Now Luisa seemed confident of the time. "It was one o'clock, of that I am sure. I look at my watch and say it is time to retire."

As Carlo and Luisa had nothing further to offer, the sergeant took his leave and consulted his list, noting that a Mr. and Mrs. James Hall lived not far away and had been notified that an officer would call sometime that morning.

"Mrs. Hall? Detective Sergeant Watkins, CID."

"Yes, please come in. My husband's not at home, but he's at his office in Grays Inn if you want to speak to him there."

"Thank you." The sergeant took the seat indicated and opened his notebook. "What can you tell me about the events of last evening, Mrs. Hall?"

"I'm afraid I can't be of much help. We attended the opera with Mrs. Renzi and Dr. Quentin and brought them to the party in our car. We were with them off and on during the course of the evening, but we had no idea anything had happened to Tina until Andrew —Dr. Quentin—called out for help."

"Have you any idea who might have wished to harm Mrs. Renzi?"

"No, I'm afraid not. You see, Andrew Quentin is our very good friend, but my husband and I didn't meet Mrs. Renzi until two days ago, so we know very little of her life except what Andrew has told us."

"Yes, I see. Did any incident occur during the course of the evening that seemed at all out of the ordinary?"

Jane paused. "There is something. When we were told you were coming this morning, my husband and I debated whether I should mention it and decided I ought to tell you about it, although it may have no significance."

"I'd be glad to hear it in any case, Mrs. Hall."

"Yes. Well, a lady named Geraldine Foster had been living with Tina's father, the composer Piero Marini, at the time he died. It was in Keswick, in the Lake District. Tina was a little girl of ten when her father accidentally drowned in the lake. Gerry Foster left England soon afterward and apparently has lived abroad for many years. Recently, I had occasion to visit Keswick to pursue research and had an unpleasant encounter with the lady." And Jane described what happened at the house by the lake.

"Now, Sergeant, Geraldine Foster was there at the party last night. She seemed perfectly normal, and when she saw Tina, she greeted her warmly, but Tina did not respond and walked away. I believe that as a child she had resented her father's attachment to Miss Foster, and twenty years later she still felt no desire to renew the acquaintance."

The sergeant looked up from his notes. "Thank you for reporting this, Mrs. Hall."

"It doesn't seem likely Miss Foster would attack Mrs. Renzi after an absence of twenty years—"

"Exactly. But if she should be in an unbalanced state?"

"Yes, I'm afraid that's why we thought we should tell you about it."

"Quite right." And thanking Jane again, the sergeant took his leave.

Detective Superintendent Fielding set his coffee cup on his desk, ran a hand through his thinning hair and stared moodily at Sergeant Watkins.

"So, Sergeant, which will you have? The boyfriend? The cousin? The ex-husband's mistress? Mamma's consort? The old school friend? The Greek artist?"

"Or the madwoman at the lake?"

"Yes. We're waiting for a report on her. It seems she went back straightaway this morning. A chap named Clifford Cox gave us her address in Keswick—that's up in Cumbria. Our man there will see her."

It was late in the afternoon, and Fielding had gathered reports from officers who had interviewed dozens of guests from the party at Hampstead, in addition to the reports from Sergeant Watkins.

"No word from the hospital, sir? The lady must be pulling through."

"Yes." Fielding's mouth twisted. "If she dies, we'll be the first to know. Whoever did it must have meant business. According to the doctor, the fellow was probably aiming for the heart, but the knife was deflected by striking a rib, and penetrated the lung instead. The danger seems to be from shock. Tests show she had been given a sedative before the stabbing, so that she didn't cry out. Whoever did it must have dropped something into her champagne glass. Lucky they found her when they did."

"I'm afraid we won't get much in the way of dabs, sir. That jeweled handle on the knife won't tell much, although our artist friend, Mr. Spyros, couldn't know that. He decided he'd better come clean about opening the cabinet and handling the knife after I asked for their fingerprints."

"Right. Our chap probably slipped on a glove in any case, or held the weapon with a handkerchief or such. He clearly wasn't worried about leaving prints, since he dropped the knife conveniently into a potted plant in the corner of the room. Of course, he could hardly be seen rejoining the party carrying a bloody knife in his hand."

"No problem with access to the weapon, sir. Anybody could lift it from that curio cabinet. A man could pop it into his pocket, or a lady into her handbag, even in those little ones they carry for evening."

"So, if it *was* attempted murder, and I don't see how it could be otherwise, who would benefit? The blonde, Mrs. Brecht, says Mamma's 'permanent other' has lost a packet of money and the victim refused to come to the rescue. But our best bet on the money side is the husband's cousin, what's his name?"

"Carlo Renzi, I believe."

"Right you are. And what about the lady with him—Luisa Valle? Both staying at the Russell. Together, do you think?"

"They had separate rooms, sir, but not far apart, I'd say. When he rang her up, she was at the door in two shakes."

"She was not weeping over the possible demise of our lady, I gather?"

"Quite the contrary. Made no secret of her dislike. Claimed Mrs. Renzi had killed 'her Mario.'"

"Curious thing that. The lady's Mamma said the same thing. Mr. Traherne explained it was in self-defense, but who was the corroborating witness? None other than the fiancé, the American professor."

"Could they have done it together?"

"The only problem with that theory is the professor had just arrived in Florence and hadn't set eyes on the lady until that day."

"And now, after two months or so, they are engaged to be married."

"So he says. Not official, mind you, but love seems to have blossomed in the warm Italian clime."

Fielding leaned back in his chair. "The professor appears devastated, but distraught lovers are prime suspects, in my experience. Chap says he was standing guard by the door to prevent anyone from disturbing his lady love and had no idea there was another door to the room."

"Right, sir, and that makes it dead easy for him to do the deed himself."

"And we mustn't forget Mamma and Mr. Traherne. While she's in the ladies', he passes by the door in the paneled wall. Easy enough to nip in and out again and nobody the wiser."

At the sound of the phone, Fielding lifted the receiver. "Yes? . . . Right, go ahead."

A few brief notes, and he said thank you and rang off.

"That was the report on the Foster woman. Claims she never attacked anyone at the lake—the lady must have been mistaken. Also, she hasn't seen Mrs. Renzi for twenty years. Was shocked to hear someone had tried to kill her. Knows nothing whatever about it. Was not surprised Tina Renzi had grown into a beautiful woman, as she was an exceptionally pretty child."

"Everyone remarks on the lady's attractions."

"Hard to tell at the moment. When I visited the hospital early this morning, the poor creature was a mass of tubes and needles."

"So what next, sir?"

"I wish I knew. You can pack it in for the weekend, Sergeant. I'll pop into the hospital tomorrow. Let's hope the case hasn't become a homicide by that time."

On Saturday morning Andrew Quentin stood quietly at the nurses' station on the floor of the hospital where Tina Renzi was a patient in the intensive care unit. The day before, he had been told she could have no visitors under any circumstances and was given a telephone number he might ring to inquire. Only the mother, Mrs. Emilia Marini, would be officially notified if there should be "any change in the patient's condition," a phrase he took to be a euphemism for "if the patient should die."

At the Traherne residence in Hampstead a manservant had taken all phone calls, and understandably declined to allow anyone to speak with Mamma. After some pleading, Andrew had succeeded in getting through to Edmund, who, after many exclamations of their distress over Tina, had promised to ring up Andrew and leave a message on his friend's machine if there were any news to report.

"It's no good my going to the hospital, dear boy," Edmund had lamented. "They won't let anyone in except the signora, and of course she is quite unable to go."

Andrew refrained from remarking that if Emilia could go to the opera, she could get to the hospital to see her daughter. None of his affair, after all.

Now, after a second night of fitful sleep, he stood silently waiting for someone to tell him more than the routine answer that "the patient is resting comfortably."

At last a starched presence appeared. "I am Sister Murphy. How may I help you?"

"I am Mrs. Renzi's fiancé. I should like to know how she is progressing."

"An American, are you?"

"Yes, Sister."

Cold, beady eyes regarded him suspiciously. "You know, of course, that Mrs. Renzi was the victim of a murderous attack? The police have instructed us to allow no visitors. When she leaves this unit, there will be a guard at the door of her room."

"Yes, I understand—" Andrew's voice broke. "I simply want to know how she is getting on."

The sister's expression softened. "In layman's terms, the lung collapsed as a result of the knife wound and is being reinflated by means of a tube. Her vital signs are improving, and the doctor believes she will fully recover."

Unable to speak, Andrew simply looked his gratitude, and the sister patted his arm. "Not to worry, sir. We'll bring her round."

A voice behind him made Andrew turn.

"I *must* speak to someone in charge. I am Signora Renzi's cousin!"

Carlo Renzi's dark eyes moved over Andrew's face with contempt. "What do you do here? You have no right—"

Sister Murphy stepped forward. "Please, sir, lower your voice. We have very sick people in this ward. I believe this gentleman is the lady's fiancé."

"That is what *he* says, but is not true. I tell you, it is not true!"

Andrew looked with some surprise at Carlo, then said quietly, "Nor is he her cousin. He is the cousin of her late husband, no relation to Mrs. Renzi herself."

"Gentlemen, please!" Detective Superintendent Fielding appeared like a genie out of a bottle. "Thank you, Sister."

The nurse moved gratefully away as Fielding ushered Andrew and Carlo down the corridor. "Now, we have good news about Mrs. Renzi this morning. Professor Quentin, I believe you have already been told that she is expected to make a full recovery?"

"Were you listening, then?"

Fielding smiled. "I happened to be standing nearby. We are naturally interested in anyone who comes to inquire about the patient." He looked at Carlo.

"Ah, I am so happy that she will survive! *Bene, bene!*"

The superintendent spoke briskly. "Now, gentlemen, since no visits to the patient are permitted, I suggest that your presence here can be of no immediate assistance."

Like schoolchildren dismissed by the teacher, Andrew and Carlo rose and walked to the lift, descending in silence. When they reached the outer door of the hospital, Andrew turned to offer his hand to Carlo and was jolted by the malice in the man's stare.

Carlo hissed, "She will not marry you!" and walked swiftly away.

• 24 •

By Monday evening Jane reported to James the good news from Andrew that Tina was improving rapidly and had been moved from the intensive care unit. As a paying patient, not on the National Health plan, she had a private room at the hospital, where Andrew had been allowed a brief visit.

"She asked for me," Andrew had said on the phone, "and Superintendent Fielding gave his permission for me to have five minutes. Not a very intimate meeting, with the constable on duty standing firmly on the other side of the bed, eyeing me with deep suspicion."

"Nevertheless, Andrew must be ecstatic," James said.

Jane frowned. "I'd have thought so, but it's odd—he sounds almost more exhausted than happy. I think he's still in a state of shock."

"Don't forget, darling, whoever tried to kill Tina may try again. Andrew's only too aware of that, I'm afraid."

"Yes, and so am I. Tomorrow morning I have an appointment to see Mr. Clifford Cox."

James raised an eyebrow. "You don't think Clifford waddled into the room and stabbed her? His motive would be a bit remote, wouldn't it?"

Jane smiled. "Yes, but he may know something that would help."

At half-past nine the next morning, Jane gave Laura a hug, said good-bye to Mrs. Lecky, her housekeeper, and set off in the nippy air of November to walk into the Strand.

Finding Mrs. Lecky was one of the happier accidents of Jane's life in London. On her walks with the infant Laura in her pram, she had chatted almost daily with a lady on the next street, who, without admitting to straitened circumstances, had agreed to occasional babysitting and housecleaning. Adoring the baby from the first, Mrs. Lecky had gradually become a regular member of the Hall ménage, coming each day from nine to one but willing to stay through the afternoon when needed. Unfortunately, her husband Jock did not approve of his wife being out at night, so Jane kept a list of sitters for their evenings out.

Now and then, if neither Jane nor James could be home by half-past five, Mrs. Lecky had taken Laura around the corner to her place while she prepared the evening meal for her husband. "Mind you, Mrs. Hall, I'd be happy to stay on, but Jock likes his supper on the table at six, don't you see?"

Much to Jane's surprise, the formidable Jock had grown fond of the baby.

"She smiled at him," Mrs. Lecky reported one day, "and he was ever so pleased."

When Laura began to call him "Dock" and put up her arms to be held, Jock was entirely won over.

Recently, when a sitter had canceled on short notice and Jane had exhausted her list, Mrs. Lecky had offered to ask Jock to break his prohibition for "just the one time." Instead, Jock had said, "Why not bring the little mite here? We can look after her."

"I'm afraid it will be rather late when we come for her," Jane had said.

"Jock says let her stay the night!"

And Laura had slept "like an angel" in the spare room, a chair against the bed as a protection against falling.

Now, as Jane walked swiftly along Long Acre and down through Covent Garden, where clusters of street stalls braved the cold, she brought her mind back to the problem of Andrew and Tina. James was right that Clifford Cox, and for that matter, Geraldine Foster, would seem to have no motive whatever for disposing of Tina, but Jane couldn't shake the feeling that something in the past might be significant. Could

Tina, at the age of ten, have seen or heard something that meant nothing to her at the time but would be seen as a threat by someone else?

The music publishing firm of Hawkins and Booth occupied two upper floors above a row of shops in the Strand, where Jane was shown into an office furnished with fine old pieces, a Turkish carpet, and an oil painting over the hearth.

Clifford Cox rose heavily from his chair, his eyes sunken in folds of flesh, and looked at her curiously.

"Miss Winfield? Please sit down. I believe you are acquainted with Mrs. Tina Renzi. Have you any information as to her condition?"

"Yes, I believe she is out of danger and doing well."

"Excellent. What a shocking thing. The police rang up the other day, but of course I knew nothing about it. They asked me for the address of the lady who came with me to the party. I believe they wished to interview all of the guests who were present." Clifford shifted his weight in his chair. "I am not certain why you wish to see me . . ."

Jane had decided to go straight to the point. "It concerns Miss Geraldine Foster, the lady you spoke of. When I was in Keswick for the interview with your mother—"

"Yes, I recall seeing you there." Clifford's tone was noncommittal.

"As I spoke with your mother, I saw you walking with Miss Foster in the garden. I had had a most distressing experience the evening before. I had gone to have a look at Lakeside, the Marini house on the lake, in connection with my work, when I encountered Miss Foster in the garden. She was in a severely disturbed state, calling to Piero Marini and crying out that his spirit was still there in the lake."

As Jane described Gerry Foster's attack on herself and her rescue by the taxi driver, Clifford listened in silence, his eyes blank.

When she had finished, he said, "Why did you not tell me this at the time?"

"After the interview with your mother, I considered speaking with you about it then, but I don't believe—"

Clifford nodded. "Yes, I quite see. I'm afraid I was rather brusque."

"The point is, when we met the other evening at the party in Hampstead, Miss Foster gave the impression that she did not recognize me. I am naturally concerned to know whether this was feigned or genuine, and whether she is likely to renew her hostility toward me in some way in the future. I am hoping you can help me." Jane wasn't at all sure Clifford would buy this story, but it was the best she could do.

Fortunately, Clifford made no objection. His swivel chair creaked as he leaned back and stretched his legs under the desk. "Miss Foster's is a curious story. I had known her before she met Marini. She was a piano teacher here in London, and we met in music circles, as one is likely to do in this business. I was rather taken with her, but because I was four or five years younger, she refused to take me seriously. She had had a disastrous marriage and had taken back her maiden name after the divorce.

"When she met Marini, he was nearly sixty and Gerry not yet forty, but it was a passionate affair from the first. Gerry and I remained friends. In fact, I rather became her confidant. We were amused by the fact that my mother was Marini's first wife. My own recollections of Marini from my childhood were vague in the extreme. When I was allowed to visit with

Mama, Marini was never unkind to me, but rather bored, I should say.

"When at last he had a child of his own, it was a different thing altogether. He used to bring the little girl into the office here from time to time—quite doted on her."

Afraid to break the spell of reminiscence, Jane said softly, "You met him here?"

"Oh, yes. In Italy, Ricordi's of Milan published all of his things, but we had everything he chose to publish in this country. A lucrative account, of course. I wasn't personally in charge, but we met from time to time. He always politely inquired about Mama. Since she was quite happily married to my stepfather, there was no awkwardness.

"But to return to Miss Foster. Poor Gerry was devastated when Marini died. Then, not long after, she went off to New Delhi with a chap who did a splendid line in exports. I heard from her now and then until the letters stopped. A few weeks ago the fellow died and Gerry came back to London and looked me up. Then she went up to Keswick and took a place on the lake for a few months. It was when I saw her there that she told me about her illness."

"Yes?"

"A sad thing. Some years ago she began having spells of blacking out, doing things she afterward knew nothing about. They consulted the best doctors, but they could do little for her until a new medication came along that does the trick so long as she remembers to take it. Sometimes, she tells me, she either forgets or goes off it because she's convinced she doesn't need it anymore, and then she may have another spell. That's what must have happened when you met her at the lake, Miss Winfield. Poor lady, when she saw you at the party, she would have no idea you had ever met, much less what she had done. She would be most distressed, I know, and such an incident is unlikely to occur again."

"I understand. Thank you so very much, Mr. Cox. You have been most reassuring."

Clifford levered himself up. "Not at all. Only too glad to be of help."

Jane stood up and held out her hand, saying casually, "During an interview with Mrs. Emilia Marini, I was told that you were acquainted with her during her marriage to Marini, and before she met Mr. Traherne."

Now Clifford's little eyes shrank into his head. "Yes, that is so," he said. "And now, if you will excuse me?"

That evening, telling James about her interview with Clifford Cox, Jane said, "Look, darling, I'd like to run up to Keswick tomorrow. Can you be home for Laura by half-past five or so?"

"My pleasure!"

"Good. I should be able to catch a late train back. If not, I'll ring you and stay over. I can take my work with me on the train."

"Do try to stay out of trouble, love. Better wear a life jacket in case you're dumped in the lake again, and please avoid walking on the fells. Remember, Andrew was nearly shoved off one of the nastier peaks."

"I promise!"

· 25 ·

ON THE 9:45 FROM EUSTON THE NEXT MORNING, JANE USED the four hours on the train to good advantage, revising and working over a piece she was doing for a monthly review journal. A mediocre sandwich on the train had passed for lunch, and by the time she picked up a hired car at Penrith and drove into Keswick, it was getting on toward three o'clock.

The evening before, Jane had asked Andrew if he thought Tina would mind if she looked over the house at the lake. "Any chance I could get inside for a look around?"

"I don't see why not. I'm sure Tina would have no objection. She spoke of a Mr. Elton, an estate agent, who looks after the place for her. He would have the keys."

In Keswick, Jane found Mr. Elton in his office. Saying that as she was in the vicinity, and had promised to pick up some items for Mrs. Renzi, she was given the keys without hesitation. "If you'll kindly return these to the office, Miss Winfield? If we are closed, just pop them through the letter drop."

At Lakeside, parking the car in the same spot where Nick had stopped his taxi, Jane studied the pair of keys, one labeled "Lake door," the other "Service door." Not keen on walking around the house into the garden, she elected to try the door facing her, at what would be the back of the house.

The key worked smoothly, and she found herself in

a large pantry, lined with shelves and cupboards, opening into one of those Victorian kitchens big enough to serve the needs of a burgeoning family and a cluster of servants.

When Piero Marini bought the house in the 1930s for his first bride, Vera, the house had no doubt been brought up to date, and it looked to Jane as though nothing had changed much since then. A gas cooker of now ancient vintage graced the wall under the chimney where a woodburning stove had once stood, and the porcelain sink showed blackened chips, the battle scars of half a century of use. Marini's second bride, the young Emilia, had grown up with servants and probably never saw the kitchen. Only a modern refrigerator, gleaming white against the gray walls, looked like an acquisition from the era of Tina's occasional uses of the house.

Idly opening the refrigerator door, Jane was surprised to see a small carton of milk, a package of scones, and some margarine, fruit, and cheese. Of course, she thought, there must be a woman who comes to clean and wants her cups of tea and a snack. Yes, there was the obligatory electric teakettle in a corner of the drainboard.

A drawer under the counter was not fully closed, and Jane gave it an automatic push, only to find it had stuck in that position. Pulling it out to try again, she noticed at the top of assorted papers a shopping list headed "Deliver to Lakeside, 14 November."

In addition to the usual basic items, the list included two fillet steaks, four lamb cutlets, half a dozen bottles of wine, and a whole chicken. Jane smiled. These must have been ordered on the day Tina arrived in Keswick, for two days later, when Andrew came, she assured him she had plenty of food in the house. Could she have suspected he might come? Or at least hoped that he might guess where she was and follow her?

This time the drawer closed, and Jane wandered out of the kitchen and into the other rooms on the ground floor of the house. In the music room she stood looking at Marini's piano, where so many of his works had been conceived, and where he had been working on the night of his death. Still a handsome and obviously virile man at seventy, he might have had many more productive years. What a difference it would have made in Tina's life to have kept the security of her father's affection through her childhood.

Shivering in the unheated house, Jane remembered it was Tina's room she had come to see, and started up the stairs. She had no idea what she might learn; she only knew she wanted to look out of that attic window and try to see what Tina had seen on the night of the tragedy.

At the top of the first flight of stairs, she followed a carpeted passage between a row of closed doors— obviously the bedrooms and baths for family and guests. At the far end of the passage she found the uncarpeted stairs leading to the attic floor and the servants' quarters, with Tina's bedroom in the center under the gable.

Jane felt a flick of sorrow at the sight of the little bed with its faded floral spread. Matching curtains were draped at each window and framed the window seat that looked out over the garden and the lake.

Remembering the testimony at the coroner's inquest, she stood by the bed, then moved to the window seat. Something woke her up, Tina had said. She couldn't sleep, so she put on a robe and sat here. She saw her father sitting at the end of the jetty. Then she went back to bed. And then she heard a splash.

A splash? Impossible! The night was cold. Her windows would be closed. She couldn't have heard a splash from the lake.

But *something* stirred her again. A different sound?

She gets up, goes to the window, and sees her father is gone. She runs down the stairs and out into the garden, but he isn't there. She runs back into the house and calls him, but he doesn't answer. Then she looks in the music room, where Gerry Foster is standing.

But *why?* Why did she assume something was wrong when Marini was no longer on the bench? Why not suppose he had simply walked back into the house?

And why not look in the music room first?

Something is missing from the child's story—but what? And why?

Sinking down on the window seat, Jane stared out at the gray surface of the lake and the weathered boards of the jetty, with the shabby bench at the end. Something someone said at the party in Hampstead floated into her mind.

And suddenly she thought she knew. As surely as if she had been there that night, she could guess what had really happened.

Her mind twenty years in the past, Jane heard no one approach the attic room until a voice cried out, "What are you doing here?" and she turned to see the tall figure of Gerry Foster standing in the doorway, her masses of auburn hair disheveled, her eyes staring at Jane.

· 26 ·

WHEN JANE PLANNED TO VISIT THE HOUSE BY THE LAKE, SHE had known she might encounter Gerry Foster again, but after what Clifford Cox had told her of the transitory nature of Gerry's illness, she had thought it unlikely that Gerry would have another spell just as she arrived.

Now, looking at the disordered hair and rumpled clothing of the woman in the doorway of the attic room, she felt choked with terror until the woman spoke.

In a quite ordinary voice, Gerry said, "Oh, sorry if I startled you. I believe we've met, have we not, but—"

Swallowing hard, Jane recovered. "Yes. I'm Jane Winfield. We were at the Traherne reception after the opera last week."

"Of course! You were with Tina Renzi and her party, I believe."

"Yes."

Gerry smiled. "Then you've every right to be here in Tina's house. I'm afraid it's I who should explain my presence!"

"No, really—"

Gerry pushed and smoothed at her abundant hair. "The fact is, I was asleep! But look here, shall I make us a pot of tea and we can talk?"

Jane followed the woman down the back stairs to the next floor and along the carpeted passage, where one of the doors now stood open.

"Look," said Gerry, pushing the door wide to

reveal a huge poster bed with an eiderdown flung back and a pillow still showing the indentation of a head. "This is where I slept when I lived here. I expect you know I was living with Piero?"

"Yes."

"I've taken a place nearby, and I come here often. This afternoon I went into my old room and fell asleep under the eiderdown. It makes me feel close to Piero, you see. Then I heard footsteps on the floor above and found you there!"

"How do you get in? Isn't the house locked?"

"Of course, but I still have my keys. No one's ever bothered to change the locks."

In the kitchen Gerry filled the electric kettle, popped two scones into the toaster, and set out the cheese and fruit.

"You see, if I have tea, it makes me feel a part of the house again." Her still lovely eyes looked wistfully at Jane.

"Hasn't anyone ever—that is . . . ?"

Gerry smiled. "Caught me red-handed? Not as yet. I had a close call last week, when the cleaner came. She was getting out of her car as I walked down the drive, and when she saw me, I came on and chatted with her a bit. Told her I was a neighbor, and so on, without mentioning my name. She's a friendly soul. Told me Mr. Elton had asked her to prepare the house, as Mrs. Renzi was coming. She saw my food in the fridge and assumed it had been ordered for Tina. She won't be back for a month!"

Filling their cups, Gerry frowned. "What is the news of Tina? I knew nothing about it until a policeman came to see me and told me what had happened."

"She's doing very well, I believe. There seems no doubt she will recover."

"Oh, how splendid! Such a beautiful young woman. She was a very pretty child. I was sorry she was so cold to me at the party the other evening. I should like to be friends, but she clearly does not wish it. She adored Piero, you see, and I believe she resented his attentions to me."

"He was fond of her too, I understand," Jane hazarded.

"Oh, absolutely doting."

Gerry fell silent, and after a moment Jane said, "You must have been sleeping very soundly this afternoon. I walked about downstairs and then along the passage past the room where you were sleeping."

Gerry responded cheerfully. "Yes. It's probably my medication," and she described her illness much as Clifford Cox had done.

"When the symptoms first appeared, some years ago," she went on, "the doctors regarded it as 'mental' and sent me to a series of psychiatrists who had me talking endlessly about my unhappy marriage and the tragedy of Piero's death. They tried desperately to dredge up traumatic events from my childhood, but they were frustrated to learn that I had grown up in a cheerful home with parents who were genuinely fond of their children.

"In the end, medical research turned up the fact that conditions like mine are caused by a chemical imbalance, and once the right medicine is found, it's possible to control it rather well. The man I lived with was wonderfully supportive, and that made all the difference for me."

Feeling confident that Gerry wouldn't know of her visit to Clifford's office, Jane decided to put out a feeler. "I believe you were with Mr. Clifford Cox at the reception last week?"

"Yes! Dear Clifford. How he has changed in twenty

175

years—all that appalling fat! He was always a bit chubby, but rather nice looking in his younger years."

"I understand he was here in Keswick at the time Mr. Marini died."

Gerry looked thoughtful. "Yes, he was, actually."

"Did he visit here at the house?"

Jane wondered if Gerry would object to these seemingly irrelevant questions, but she seemed to enjoy reminiscing about the past.

"No, no, not here! Piero couldn't abide him. He knew Clifford had been begging me to marry him before Piero and I met, and he was violently jealous. It was quite irrational—I'd never really cared for Clifford, except as a friend, but men can be so absurd. They seem to think a woman can switch her affections as quickly as she changes a frock!"

Some can, Jane thought, but that can be said of both sexes.

Keeping her tone level, Jane went on. "It must have been dreadful for you when Piero Marini died."

Gerry stared down at her teacup. "Yes, it was." As if she were compelled to relive the tragedy, she described in detail what had happened that night. "You see, it was so sudden, so unexpected. That's why I like to come here to the house. I feel in touch with Piero here."

Jane's breath shortened; she remembered only too well Gerry's communing with the spirit of her dead lover.

Then, quite suddenly, Gerry smiled. "But tell me about yourself, Miss Winfield." And she listened with what seemed to be genuine interest to Jane's mention of her writing, her husband, and her infant daughter.

"And how do you happen to be in Keswick, Miss Winfield?"

Was the question as innocent as it sounded? Jane repeated the story she had given Mr. Elton, the estate agent, about picking up some items for Tina while passing through.

"And did you find what you were looking for?"

Jane patted the capacious tote bag at her side and stood up, hoping to give the impression it contained whatever Tina had asked for. "Yes, I have it all. Thank you so much for the tea, Miss Foster. I must be off."

As she drove back toward the village, she could still see the odd look on Gerry Foster's face. Jane knew there weren't many items lying around the house to make her story plausible, but it was the best she could do.

What Gerry didn't know was that now she was certain her guess was right. She *had* found what she came for.

By half-past ten that evening, Jane curled up on the sofa with James's arm around her, reporting the events of the day. After leaving Gerry Foster at Lakeside, she had sped back to Penrith and managed to catch a train that deposited her at Euston by ten o'clock.

"So, darling, does my theory make sense to you, or am I being fanciful?"

James cleared his throat. "I'm afraid it's all too likely. The question is, what can we do? It's not exactly the kind of evidence the police would find convincing, even if we wanted to go to them with it."

"It was all so long ago. . . ."

"Yes, although there's no statute of limitations on murder, love."

"The thing is, would it benefit anyone at all to dredge it up now?"

"Let sleeping dogs lie?"

"I suppose that's what I mean."

Suddenly, Jane sat up. "But there *is* something that might have a bearing on the present. When I go to Lucerne on Saturday, I could take a small side trip."

James looked at her speculatively. "In the direction of Lake Brienz, perhaps?"

Jane nodded. "Yes, darling, that's what I had in mind."

On the evening of their dinner with Andrew and Tina, Jane had had no idea she would be going to Switzerland so soon. When Tina spoke of her visit to Lake Brienz, Jane had thought vaguely that she and James might consider the Alps for the following summer.

Then the editor of a music journal to whom she had submitted a proposal had shown strong interest. The project, a series of articles on pianists who had won major competitions and what they were doing some years later, required tracking down her chosen subjects and doing interviews with each. One of these was doing a concert in Lucerne before taking off for an extended tour of the Far East, and she had decided to catch him before he got away.

On the flight to Zurich that morning the air was clear, giving a spectacular view of the snowcapped mountains, but by the time she took the train to Lucerne, the peaks had retreated behind blanketing clouds. Dropping her bag at the hotel, she walked back to the station in time for a local train which stopped at Brienz on the way to Interlaken.

Patchy snow laced the ground as the train passed Lake Lucerne, the white carpet becoming thicker as they climbed sharply along sides of mountains, with valleys below and villages tucked at the foot of hills rising on the opposite side. After an hour or so they descended to a broader valley, passing through the little town of Meiringen and presently coming to the tip of Lake Brienz. Not far along the side of the lake lay the village of the same name. The mountain behind rose so sharply that the town had little choice but to straggle along between the wooded slopes and the lake.

Jane stepped off the train and walked through the small station. Across the road stood the bright red cars of a funicular. Hadn't Tina mentioned to Andrew taking the "cable" up the mountain? The sign informed her that an hour would take the passenger to the top of the Rothorn, close to eight thousand feet elevation, but with another hour back, there simply wasn't time today. Maybe, if she and James came in the summer . . .

Remembering Tina's remarks at dinner that evening in London, Jane thought there was a chance at least of finding the place where Tina had stayed as a child when she came to Brienz with her parents. She had no idea what she could learn, but the thought haunted her that something may have happened to make this a place of special significance to Tina. Finding herself so near, she couldn't pass up the chance to try. If nothing came of it, she would at least have a pleasant side trip.

Not far along the main street, she saw the tourist information office and asked for a map of the town, then followed the road as it wound along, bordered with small chalet-style hotels and inns. A few side streets wandered down toward the lake on one side and up the base of the mountain on the right until the quick ascent precluded further habitation. A ten minute walk brought her to the end of the village. Jane was sure that Tina, when she ran away from Florence in fear, would have returned to the place where she had stayed as a child. But how to find it? Nothing to do but turn back. Short of asking after Tina at each one of the dozen or two hotels, there was little clue to which one it might be.

Better to try the esplanade along the quay. Back at the station she walked down to the boat landing, deserted now in the off-season, and turning right, followed the gravel path that skirted the edge of the lake.

Instead of the sky-blue lake she had more or less expected, Lake Brienz was pure turquoise, a beguiling blue-green that gleamed even under the overcast skies. Long and narrow, the lake lay between nearly vertical cliffs, so that, looking across the water, she saw the sharp rise of the precipice, heavily wooded, and patched with outcroppings of stone.

On her right, as she followed the path by the lake, stood some fine old houses, most appearing to be private residences, but a few bearing a discreet sign indicating hotel accommodations.

Not far along a bend in the path, she stopped abruptly. Directly in front of her, on a raised pedestal, was the charming statue of a young woman, reclining on one arm, her hair in two braids over her breasts, her sheer dress revealing the delicate lines of her body.

"A statue dedicated to some poet," Tina had said that night at dinner.

Engraved at the base of the figure, Jane read: *Dem Dichter Albert Streich,* and the dates, 1897–1960.

Yes, her German from school days told her, *Dichter* meant poet. And below the name were the words Tina had mentioned: *Gestiftet von den Brienzerfrauen.* A gift from the women of Brienz.

Now Tina's words came back to her. "Just below our chalet was a statue . . ."

From where she stood, Jane scanned the houses along the quay and saw nothing to indicate rooms available. Possibly one of these had been a hotel more than twenty years ago but was now a private home. Perhaps a little farther along. Sure enough, after a bend in the gravel path beyond the statue, Jane saw a house with an inn sign.

May as well try, she thought, ringing the bell.

A plump woman of about forty opened the door, and in answer to Jane's question, said yes, she spoke English a little.

"Can you tell me if an Italian lady, Mrs. Renzi, stayed here about a month ago?"

"Please to come in."

"Thank you."

In the welcome warmth of the reception lounge, Jane waited while the woman looked through the register.

"Ah, yes, Frau Renzi! Of course, a very beautiful young lady."

That was Tina, all right. "I wonder if Frau Renzi might have stayed at this same hotel when she was a child?"

The woman pondered. "Yes. I believe she tell me she come with her father and mother when she is a little girl. She ask for the people who were landlords then, but I do not know them. My husband and I have been here since fifteen years."

Well, it had been a long shot. She had found the place, but no one who might have told her about the past.

About to take her leave, Jane was jolted by words she never expected to hear.

Smiling, the woman said, "Such a handsome couple! The gentleman come soon after Frau Renzi arrive and must leave early."

Who on earth? To ask for a description of the man might sound odd. Then Jane remembered the time-honored ploy and said casually, "A tall, fair-haired man?"

Surprised, the woman said, "No." And she described the man who had been with Tina for a part of the week.

• 27 •

AT CASA MARINI, TINA RECLINED ON A SOFA IN THE SHADowy sitting room, the massive dark furniture glowering over her fragile figure. At her side, Andrew took her white hand in his. "Now you must talk to me, Tina. No more evasions."

And she whispered, "Yes, I know."

It was Sunday morning, the tenth day after the attack on Tina at the party in Hampstead. The English doctor looking after her had announced on Friday that she would be released from the hospital the next day, and she had said at once she wanted to come back to Florence.

"I feel perfectly well," she had insisted. "Only a little tired."

Then she had shocked Andrew by stating that Carlo Renzi would go with her on the plane. "He's making such a fuss, darling, it's simply not worth arguing with him. Don't you see?"

Andrew had not seen at all, but conceded that now

was not the time to make things more difficult for her. He had taken a later plane into Pisa and come to Casa Marini in the evening, learning from Luigi that Tina had already retired for the night, and listening patiently to the old servant's lamentations on what had happened to the signora.

"She's doing very well now, Luigi," Andrew soothed. "She should be perfectly well in no time."

He had hoped Tina might come to his room in the night—not to make love, simply to let him hold her, comfort her—but she had not come.

Now he said firmly, "What is the problem with Carlo?"

Tina's eyes swam with tears. "Oh, Andrew, I don't know what to do. Carlo says he is in love with me. He wants to marry me. He seems to have gone quite mad."

"But has he any reason to believe you care for him?"

"No! We were always on friendly terms when I was married to Mario, and after the separation, I think I knew then he would have liked to—well, to be with me. But I never encouraged him!"

"Then I don't quite see what right he has—"

"He has no right! But he knows now about us, and he's insane with jealousy. He said he didn't know until the night of the party. He thought you were just somebody doing research on Babbo's papers. Then he told me he came into the doorway of the little room where we had had our food. He saw you kiss me and heard me say I loved you. Oh, Andrew, I'm so afraid!"

"But darling, it's the twentieth century. He can't make you marry him if you don't want to."

"He said he believed I would have come to care for him if you hadn't come along."

"What about the three years you were separated from Mario? If he hadn't convinced you by that time, why now?"

"Well, he was involved with someone else for a lot of that time. It was only lately that he sort of came back to wanting me again."

"There's only one thing to do, Tina. Tell him to get lost, and if you don't, I will."

Tina shuddered. "You don't understand. He is full of violence, just as Mario was, and I'm afraid—"

"That he will attack you?"

"No! I'm afraid for *you*. He told me yesterday he would kill you before he would let me marry you!"

"I wouldn't take that too seriously, darling. He won't want to spend years in prison just to get rid of me."

"You don't know him, Andrew. He's half out of his mind. You can't possibly stay here now. It's too dangerous. I told him you would leave in a few days."

Now Andrew's temper flared. "Oh, I see. And where am I going?"

"Well, I thought, to a hotel?"

"And what would prevent him from tracking me down and murdering me there, may I ask?"

Tears sprang from Tina's eyes and made rivulets on her pale cheeks. "Please, darling, it's not my fault!"

Andrew's anger fizzled and died. "No, I suppose not. I saw Carlo at the hospital in London one day, and I have to admit he looked daggers at me and made some crack about how you would never marry me, but I hardly imagined he was thinking in terms of murder. I'll have a talk with him."

"No, don't! That would only enrage him more."

"You're probably right. But look, this is bound to blow over if we give it time. Before long, he'll see that you really don't care for him. At that point, he'll have to give up."

"I suppose so."

"There's just one thing, darling. You're sure he won't attack *you?* What if he turns his rage on you when you turn him down?"

"No, I'm sure he won't. It's you he hates."

"I see. Well, I'm not leaving here, whatever you say. We'll wait and see if he backs off, and if he doesn't, we'll both leave. We can simply go to California, darling. Surely he won't follow us there."

Tina frowned. "I don't know what he might do."

At lunchtime the late November rain darkened the sky. Luigi served their meal in the dining room, where yellow lights from the chandelier only partially dispelled the gloom. They ate in near silence, neither wanting to talk about Carlo, and equally unable to find solace in small talk.

Andrew looked at Tina's drooping face and remembered past occasions with mingled pain and joy. The first time they lunched here, when he knew he was in love but had no clue to Tina's feelings. The day she looked so troubled and fled from the table, saying she was afraid someone was trying to kill her. The day she glowed with pleasure when Andrew said, "Let's go to Venice."

And now there were no words between them.

At the end of the meal Tina said, "I must rest, darling."

"Yes, of course. Will you come to the workroom for coffee? I'll tell Luigi four o'clock, shall I?"

"Yes, please."

Stretched out on his bed, Andrew wondered how serious Carlo was about actually killing him. Probably just a threat, he decided, in the hope Tina would give up on what might be a passing infatuation.

More important than the crisis with Carlo was Andrew's fear, not expressed to Tina, that the unknown assailant who had attacked her at the party in Hampstead would try again. Whoever it was must have waited for a time when plenty of people were around in order to avoid detection, and would now be waiting till another chance came along. All the more reason to get her safely away.

When Luigi had delivered the coffee to the workroom at four o'clock, and Tina came in moments later, Andrew took her in his arms and held her against him, his throat thick with pain.

"I want to take care of you, Tina. Soon we must go home to California where I can look after you. Will you do that?"

"Yes—as soon as we can."

Tina sank onto the sofa by the piano, and Andrew poured their coffee and took the chair at her side. Silence fell between them, as it had over lunch, each sitting like a stone figure in a museum.

I can't bear this, Andrew thought, but I have no power to change it.

A knock at the workroom door broke the spell, and Susie Brecht burst into the room, followed by Luigi bearing another cup and saucer.

"Tina! Why didn't you tell me you were back?"

Susie kissed Tina, then Andrew, as Tina murmured, "I meant to call you, Susie, but I just got back yesterday."

"Yes, all right. So how are you feeling?"

"Really fine. Just a little tired."

"You look awful!" Susie said briskly. "Andrew, is she really all right?"

"Yes, truly. The doctors said once the lung was

reinflated, she should have no further trouble. It's just a matter of healing."

"Thank God for that. So what's with you two? You look like something out of a Bela Lugosi film."

"It's Carlo. You won't believe this." Tina regained some animation as she poured out the story to Susie.

"He must be out of his mind, all right." Susie frowned. "He nailed me at the party that night and asked me if you were in love with Andrew, but I never imagined this was the reason. He went on with some stuff about being the head of the Renzi family. When I said Tina could do as she liked, he turned all smiles and said, of course I was right, or something like that. He must have been covering up, the skunk."

Tina's mouth trembled. "What can we do, Susie?"

"Well, for openers, I'd say you'd better not stick around here too long."

Andrew said, "You think he's really dangerous, then?"

"Yes. Those Renzi guys don't just play pattycake."

A silence fell, broken by Susie with a change of subject. "You'll never guess who's coming to town— Bill, the old faithful."

Tina smiled wanly. "Oh, Susie, I hope you'll be nice to him."

Susie grinned. "Sure I will." Then, to Andrew, "Bill's the New York stockbroker my family has selected as my ideal mate. Actually, he's an extremely nice guy. I saw a lot of him when I was home last time. To tell the truth, this may be a good time for him to arrive."

"Why is that?"

"I think the great romance with Alex may be winding down. He's been off sketching here and there without showing me his work, as he'd normally do. When we went to London before the opera, he darted off for a couple of days and came back with a smug look on his face but no drawings. He acts for all the world like a guy whose mind is somewhere else, not on little Susie."

Andrew said, "Sorry to hear that."

"Thanks." Susie shrugged. "But back to your problem, Tina. Listen, why don't I move in here with you for a week or so, till Carlo calms down? Bill can drop in here and take us out."

Andrew nodded. "Good idea!"

But Tina stared at Susie with haunted eyes. Then she struggled to her feet. "It's wonderful of you to offer, Susie, but no. Thanks anyway. You see, I'm so tired. I don't feel like going anywhere, and I just need to rest until this all blows over. I'm going to lie down again. Please stay and talk to Andrew."

Waving away Andrew's offered arm, Tina walked quickly to the door.

• 28 •

WHEN SUSIE WAS GONE, ANDREW WANDERED BACK TO HIS room and stood at the far window, where lights were already coming on in the city below. A lot of things he really didn't want to think about jostled in his head and were pushed out by the overwhelming pain of memories of his wife.

He pressed his hands against his eyelids, but he couldn't shut out the insistent flashes, the vivid scenes of trivia from their days together. He saw Norma bending over a carton, trying to push down the lid, her short dark curls sticky with sweat, muttering, "Blasted thing won't stay down." He saw her as she stood at her easel and bent her head to mix a color on the palette; and at the glimpse of the soft skin at the back of her neck, he felt the instant turn-on that never failed. He heard her bubbly voice saying, "I don't want to cook, do you?" and heard himself replying, "There's the new Chinese place."

A deep, dry sob rose and seized his chest, squeezing till animal sounds broke from him. He wanted her back, here, now. Like his friend who had lost a leg in Vietnam and could never shake the amputee's belief that he would wake up one morning whole again, Andrew was assailed once more with the old familiar obsession that his wife hadn't *really* died, that some day she would be back and everything would be the same.

Impossible to stand here, letting his agony consume him. He put on a hooded jacket and strode out into the rain, walking rapidly up to the main road, following streets at random, finally easing some of the pain through sheer physical motion.

Why now? Why this spasm of grief? Well, why not? It had been happening ever since she died, and probably always would. Whatever direction his life took, this was going to happen from time to time, and he might as well face it. Eventually the intensity would fade, that's all.

Back at Casa Marini, he showered and put on slacks and a sweater, meeting Tina in the dining room for a light supper. No silence this time, he decreed, and chatted amiably about incidents from his childhood, friends in Los Angeles, anything at all to avoid referring to the crisis that faced them.

Afterward, he put Tina on the sofa in the workroom

and played a random selection of items on the piano, from a Bach partita to Chopin, Brahms, and a sonata by Marini that produced a wan smile, ending with some Cole Porter oldies that he knew she liked.

Having stalled as long as he reasonably could, he finally went to her and took her hand.

Tina sat up, her eyes looking into his then dropping to her lap, the exquisite lines of her face, with downcast eyes, recalling the tender countenance of the San Miniato madonna.

Andrew's heart twisted, and, helping her to her feet, he put his arm around her and walked her through the workroom and across the entry to the foot of the stairs.

Tina stopped and put her face up to be kissed, like a child at bedtime.

"No, I'll take you to your room."

Tina hesitated for a moment, than made no objection, and they went slowly up the stairs and along the passage to a large bedroom overlooking the terrace. Since Tina had always come to him, Andrew had never had occasion to visit her room. He found it charmingly messy, with garments tossed over the backs of chairs, shoes and slippers scattered about, and the dressing table cluttered with bottles and jars and wineglasses.

"Look, Tina, I'm staying with you tonight. It's too late to worry about appearances."

Startled, she drew back. "No! Really, I'm all right. I'll rest better if I'm alone. Honestly, darling . . ."

Andrew looked at her pale face. "All right, then, but I'll come up in the morning if you're not down."

Now the good night kiss. "Sleep well, dearest." And Andrew retraced his steps to his own room.

* * *

Tina might sleep well, Andrew thought wryly, but *he* certainly couldn't. Tossing, turning, dozing, pacing, it was no good. Too many questions haunted him, things that didn't make sense, things that only she could answer.

At midnight, the witching hour, he threw on a warm robe and walked out onto the terrace. The rain had stopped, and sidestepping shallow puddles in his slippers, he stood looking out at the faint lights below. City of art, city of power. Michelangelo and the Medicis. Nothing much had changed in human nature since the Renaissance—nor before it, for that matter. Artists like Piero Marini might make money as their fame advanced, but it had obviously meant to Marini only the comfort to work without distraction, as it did for most artists. For those who came after, the money was more likely to be a ticket to the good life.

Most of the terrace chairs and tables had been taken in against the rain, but one folding chair stood near the door to the house, and Andrew sat there for a quarter of an hour or so, breathing the rain-freshened air and trying to block out the thoughts that tortured him.

Presently, he heard a window open above him. Tina's voice, faint but clear, saying in Italian, "Look, *caro mio,* the rain's stopped," and an answering murmur in a lower register. Then Tina again, "You'd better go now."

Quietly, Andrew stepped into the house and stood in the shadow of a tall, carved cabinet, from where he saw the man who descended the stairs and let himself out of the front door of the house, a man he recognized.

Andrew's first impulse, to leap up the stairs and confront Tina, to demand answers to his questions, gave way in a moment to a deep reluctance to see her. The only questions that mattered were now already answered. Better to say nothing. Tomorrow he would leave Florence, and maybe some day the memory would fade.

Toward early morning Andrew had at last fallen into a miserable, dream-haunted sleep. He woke later than he had intended. Not wanting food, but desperate for coffee, he rang for Luigi and was dressed when the tray arrived. Gulping down his second cup, he plunged out the side door of the annex and strode up the hill, away from Casa Marini. The last remnants of the rain had dried up, but the cold wind was a reminder that even Italians have winter like everyone else, and that December was only days away.

Twenty minutes later his resolve was clear. He would pack up, telling Tina he thought he should get away from Carlo after all.

As he approached the annex, he heard music from the workroom and stopped, transfixed, then moved slowly into the room, where Tina sat at the piano, playing and singing the Coleridge song. As she reached the line "The lark is so brimful of gladness and love," she saw Andrew and stopped.

"Good morning, darling!" Tina was radiant. "Come sing it with me!"

And she began with the first words of the song, "You ask what the birds say? The sparrow, the dove?"

Then, seeing Andrew standing silent and unmoving, she broke off. "I asked Luigi to tell me when you were up! I have good news. Carlo rang up this morning and has promised to talk things over with you!"

Andrew felt no anger, only an enormous swelling agony that choked him.

Tina noticed nothing, her eyes glittering, uncomprehending. "I'm sure it's going to be all right. You're so clever, darling. You can make him understand!"

He heard her sweet voice as she went on with the song: "In the winter they're silent, the wind is so strong . . ."

Moving at last, Andrew walked to the piano and put his hands on her shoulders. "Please stop, Tina."

Surprised, she turned and nestled her head against his chest.

Then a car door slammed and Tina cried out, "He's here. Let's go out to the terrace!"

Carlo Renzi came through the house and walked toward Andrew, while Tina stood to one side, her eyes opaque.

His darkly handsome face impassive, Carlo gestured toward the garden. "If you please . . . ?"

Together the two men went down the terraced steps to the bottom of the garden, where they stood near the wall, Carlo with his hands behind his back, looking at Andrew but saying nothing.

Andrew looked up and saw Tina standing at the top of the steps beside the stone bench, where he had stood on the day he arrived at Casa Marini, only this time he was at the bottom, facing the cousin of the man who had been killed.

Ever since the night before, when he recognized Carlo Renzi as the man who came down the stairs from Tina's room, he had expected that a confrontation like this one was in the cards, and now he was ready for it.

He waited, and saw that Carlo seemed to be waiting too. At last Carlo said, "Tina tells me you wish to speak with me."

Without inflection, Andrew said, "No, I was told that it was you who wanted to talk to me."

Suddenly, at a scream from Tina, they both looked up, to see her running wildly down the steps, a knife in her hand.

A few feet away from Andrew, she shrieked, "Watch out, Andrew, he has a knife!" And with a quick motion, she handed Andrew the knife she carried. "Here, kill him, Andrew, *kill him!"*

Andrew saw Carlo reach into his pocket, and in a flash his arm was raised above him, a knife clutched firmly in his hand. Looking straight into Carlo's eyes, Andrew flung away the knife Tina had given him. Both men watched it fall into the barren shrubbery on the garden level above.

A moment later a vicious blow just under his ribs sent him to the ground, doubled up and gasping for breath. He remembered playing football in high school and being hit like this, losing consciousness in the same sickening way. The worst part was coming back to awareness, unable to breathe, and feeling that if air didn't come into his lungs pretty soon, it would be all over.

When breath did come back, in painful gulps, he rolled to one side, waiting for his eyes to focus, and what he saw filled him with horror.

Tina's body lay on the flagstone, blood pouring from multiple wounds in her chest and trickling from the side of her half-open mouth. Her inert body, her open eyes glazed, left little doubt that she was dead. Struggling to rise, Andrew saw that Carlo had thrown himself beside Tina, cradling her in his arms, blood soaking his shirt.

Sobbing and moaning, Carlo poured out fragments of grief and rage.

"Amata mia!" he cried. Then a phrase that Andrew took to be the equivalent of "How could you?"

Luigi came running, took one horrified look and

shouted that he was going for help. Andrew knew there was no hope, but let him go. The police would have to be called in any case.

Oblivious to Andrew's presence, Carlo went on. "I kill for you, and then you try to leave me! No one can love you as I have loved you."

Now Andrew saw Carlo's eyes turn to him, with a look that conveyed no hatred, only despair.

Then Carlo said, in English, "You could not have her, signore. Do I not tell you? Never. She was mine!"

As Andrew quietly got to his feet and started up the steps of the garden, he heard Carlo sobbing again and heard a word he couldn't for a moment place.

"Strega!" Carlo cried over and over. *"Strega!"*

And then Andrew remembered what *strega* meant. Witch. Sorceress.

And sorrow overwhelmed him.

• 29 •

IT WAS THURSDAY, THREE DAYS AFTER TINA'S DEATH, when Andrew finally made it back to London. When the police had come to Casa Marini, Carlo had frankly admitted to the murder, stating with sobs that Tina had been unfaithful to him, and getting soulful looks of comprehension from the uniformed officer who was the first to arrive.

Taking his cue, Andrew had acknowledged that he had indeed made love with the signora, unaware of her prior commitment to Signor Renzi.

At the Questura Polizia, the same Vice Questor who had investigated Mario Renzi's death listened carefully to Andrew's story, from which all details were omitted, and nodded. "She was a very beautiful woman. One understands. A great tragedy, is it not?"

Carlo was taken into custody and summoned his lawyers, and at last, after signing a statement, Andrew was allowed to leave. Only if Carlo should rescind his confession would Andrew be required to return and give evidence, an unlikely occurrence at best.

On Thursday morning at Heathrow, Andrew had loaded his bags and boxes into a taxi and in due course deposited them at his friend's flat, going straight on to see Jane, who was expecting him.

"Oh, Andrew! We're so sorry!" Her arms around him, she kissed his cheek. "Are you sure you want to talk about it?"

"Yes, absolutely. I need you, Jane. There are so many things I don't understand. If you weren't here, I think I'd have to abandon all my principles and look up a shrink."

"Okay, then, come and sit down. I asked Mrs. Lecky to take Laura out in the pram and give her lunch at her house, which they both seem to think a great treat. So we've got a couple of hours free."

Jane brought a tray with coffee and curled up at the other end of the sofa from Andrew, who said, "I don't know where to start."

"Start with how you feel."

"Yes. I feel terribly sad, horrified whenever I think of her lying there on the flagstones, blood pouring out everywhere. But—can you understand this, Jane?—I don't feel *loss*. When Norma died, it was like a whole chunk of myself was gone. I kept thinking, I've *lost* her, I must get her back."

"Yes. What you feel now is that somehow you're glad it's all over, is that it?"

Needles pricked Andrew's eyes. "Yes. I'm glad she

can't hurt anyone again, because in the end she would have hurt herself even more."

"It wasn't a total shock, was it? You've been uneasy for a while."

"That's right. It's only now I realize that doubts were there and I pushed them under the rug. It goes back even to the first time she told me about the threat to her life. She was never afraid in the right ways, or at the right times."

"Tell me about it."

"We were at lunch at Casa Marini. I knew something was bothering her, and at first she wouldn't say what it was. Then, just as she left the room, she said she thought someone was trying to kill her. And a few hours later, she was gone."

"Was that when she went to Switzerland?"

"Yes."

"There's something I must tell you about that, Andrew. It might help to sort out what was actually going on. You know I got back from Lucerne on Sunday. What I didn't tell you was that when I arrived there on Saturday, I went to Brienz. I found the chalet where Tina stayed that week, and the woman there described the man who spent part of the week with her. It was Carlo."

"I see. Not surprising now, is it?"

"It wasn't at all what I expected, Andrew. I want you to know I didn't intend to spy on Tina. She had gone there as a child with her parents, and I had thought something might have happened there that would have a bearing on her father's death. Finding out about Carlo was a total surprise."

"They were very keen to keep it all a secret. On the day she left Florence, Carlo came to the house and made a fuss about where she had gone."

"Yes, that must have been planned to confirm that

he didn't know where she was. Evidently, he joined her the next day in Brienz."

Andrew paused. "It was when she came back that I first felt doubts nibbling away in a dark corner of my consciousness, but that was when—that was the night she first came to my room. During that week she gave no sign of being frightened. It was as if she had forgotten about the threats. When I asked her, she said it had probably all been a joke."

"But she had taken it seriously enough to run off to Switzerland for a week."

"Yes, that was the kind of thought I buried away somewhere. Then, we had the weekend in Venice. Oh, God, Jane, I adored her. I was mad about her! But it always bothered me that she would never confide in me. On the evening before we left, as we were getting out of the gondola, she thought she saw someone she knew and was really frightened. Then, when she saw she was mistaken, no more fear. Now I understand— she thought it was Carlo, and she knew he mustn't find out about us."

"What about in the following week, before she came here to England?"

"Again, no more fear. Suddenly, that morning, she claimed there had been another phone call. The voice was supposed to have said, 'This time I mean it. *Morte!*' Why the mixture of English and Italian? That must be when I began to think there hadn't really been any threats at all, that she was leaving for some other reason. But it didn't make sense, so I buried it."

"Yes, now it would seem that the threats were created because Carlo was insisting she go away with him."

"But when I went to Keswick and found her at Lakeside, Carlo wasn't there."

Jane looked into his eyes. "Are you sure, Andrew?"

"How do you mean?"

"You told me that when you arrived at the house, there was a delay before Tina came to the door. Then she stood in the doorway until you asked to come in."

"Yes?"

"And then she said, 'Let's go into town,' and ran upstairs to get her jacket. I was in Keswick last week, and I have something more to tell you about that, but the pertinent thing here is that I ran across a food order that Tina must have called in when she arrived, asking for two steaks, four lamb cutlets, a whole chicken, and so on."

"I see. That sounds more like food for two than for one."

"Exactly. I wondered at the time if she had hoped you would come, but now I believe Carlo was there. When she went upstairs, she warned him you had come so that he could make his escape while you were in the village."

"Well, if Carlo was there, then he must have hung around and spied on us. In that case, it was Carlo who tried to shove me off the cliff."

"Yes, definitely. The trouble with this whole great theory is that if Carlo and Tina really did care for each other, why on earth keep it from everyone, and especially from you? One might say that Tina fell in love with you—and I believe she really did care for you, Andrew—and wanted to keep it from Carlo. But what we are seeing is that Carlo was just as anxious to keep you, or anyone else, from knowing about *them*. It doesn't make sense."

"I think it does now, Jane. There was something I didn't tell the police, because Carlo would only deny it, and my word would mean nothing. But when he was weeping over Tina's body, he said something that shocked me.

"My Italian may not be the greatest, but there's no doubt what he said: *I killed for you!*"

" 'I killed for you!' " Jane echoed the words. "But what did he mean?"

"He killed Mario for her."

"Mario? But you were there, Andrew—you saw Tina kill her husband in self-defense."

"I saw her stab at a stocky man with dark wavy hair, wearing a red-and-green-checked shirt."

"Carlo?"

"Yes. I believe they set me up."

"As an unimpeachable witness. Yes, you would be. You had just arrived, had never seen any of the parties before—"

"Exactly. I think Carlo was waiting in the shrubbery in the corner of the garden, and when Tina saw me appear on the terrace, she clasped her hands together and appeared to be gazing into space. I think that was the signal for Carlo to come so they could go into their act."

"How did they know you would be there?"

"Tina had asked me to come at eleven o'clock. Then Anna was told to have me wait on the terrace. Any stranger would go out by the stone bench to look down at the city, it's almost automatic."

"What if you had been late?"

"They would simply have waited until I did arrive."

"Of course. And you never did get a close look at the man who went over the wall?"

"That's right. There was a strong family resemblance between the two cousins, as everyone remarked. When the police showed me a picture of Mario Renzi, and Tina had already stated he was her husband, I naturally believed that was the man I had seen."

Jane pondered. "The body was found in the dense shrubbery below the wall. How did they get the body there?"

"I think Carlo probably got Mario to go there with him on some pretext, perhaps to meet Tina. She had played there as a child and shown it to Mario, so he would believe she might be there. Carlo must have caught Mario by surprise and stabbed him there, perhaps not long before I arrived, so that the time of death would not be too far off, in case someone found him fairly soon."

"Yes. If he had killed Mario elsewhere and brought the body there, it would have been much riskier. So, what about motive? Certainly, Carlo was mad about Tina and would have done anything for her. What did she gain from all this?"

"I think she hated her husband. She told me he refused to divorce her, but I wonder now if that was true. She may simply have wanted all his money."

"Didn't she already have plenty from her father?"

Andrew smiled bitterly. "She said herself one day that people always want more. Have you ever noticed that wealth is entirely relative? To some people I would be the affluent professor, living the good life, while to others I would be an object of pity—'How on earth does he manage on that pittance?'"

"Yes, how true. Now, if she and Mario had divorced, he would have wanted to marry his Luisa, and Tina would end up with an allowance of some kind. I hate to say it, Andrew, but getting rid of him must have seemed the best way out, especially with Carlo ready and willing to help."

Suddenly Jane stopped, saying gently, "I mustn't talk about Tina this way. Please forgive me."

"No, Jane, this is what I need, don't you see? I swing from pity to anger and back again, but what I felt for Tina was mad infatuation, not love. How could I truly love her when she was never straight with me? Everything was a lie, from beginning to end, but I made excuses. Now I need to face it, all of it!"

Jane put her hand on his arm. "One thing wasn't a lie, Andrew. Tina did care for you, I know that. Don't you see, that's what caused all the trouble with Carlo? He said, 'I killed for you,' and then she tried to leave him. In the beginning you *were* just their witness, until Tina fell in love with you."

"Yes, at least she came to prefer me to Carlo, if you call that love."

Jane flinched at the bitterness in his voice. Then, in the matter-of-fact tone he needed, she went on, "Now we know why Tina and Carlo tried so hard to conceal their relationship. If they had presented themselves to the world immediately after Mario's death as a devoted couple, even the police might have had a suspicious quiver. I suspect they planned to wait a few months and then let it be known that love had dawned."

"They certainly put it over on Luisa, that's clear. She would never have been so chummy with Carlo if she had known. By the same token, Tina kept Carlo in the dark about me. At first it must have been easy. They had to be nice to me because I was their witness. She could be seen chatting with me, going about Florence in a friendly way, meeting her friends, and so on. Carlo would have no idea of her nocturnal visits to me in the annex, while all those afternoons when they were supposedly sorting out Mario's estate they must have had their romantic interludes."

"But Andrew, what happened at the party in

Hampstead? It must have been Carlo who tried to kill her then, but why?"

"Tina said that's when he found out about me. But now it seems he suspected the truth when I arrived at the lake. He certainly followed us that day, and tried to shove me off the cliff. Then when he saw us together at the party and heard her tell me she loved me, it was too much for him."

"So she knew all along it was Carlo who stabbed her. No wonder she was depressed when you got back to Casa Marini. Now she was really stuck. If she didn't stay with Carlo, he would either kill her or reveal their murder of Mario and send them both to prison."

Andrew got to his feet and walked over to the piano, where he sat, playing the opening bars of the Coleridge song. He looked at Jane and said quietly, "This is the part I haven't told you yet. On the morning of her death, Tina was suddenly wildly elated. I was packing up the car, and she came into the workroom and started singing the love song, exactly as if nothing was wrong."

"What was she so excited about?"

"She had worked out her problem. She would use me to get rid of Carlo!"

· 30 ·

AT THE SOUND OF THE BUZZER, JANE OPENED THE DOOR TO
Mrs. Lecky holding Laura while Andrew helped stow
the pram in its accustomed place in the entry to the
flat.

After a report on Laura's lunch—"Ate like a little
lamb, she did"—Mrs. Lecky took her leave, and
Laura held out her arms to Andrew, squealing with
pleasure.

Watching Andrew and the baby together, Jane reflected that for all his gentle nature, Andrew had
plenty of inner strength. He was a survivor, and Tina's
death, tragic as it was, would not damage him irrevo-
cably.

Presently, with casual efficiency, Andrew took the
naptime bottle Jane had prepared and went off to the
nursery with Laura, who regarded Uncle Andrew as a
fully qualified family member, second only to Daddy
among her male courtiers.

When Andrew came back, Jane said, "I'll make us
some sandwiches in a minute, but tell me first. Tina
tried to use you to get rid of Carlo?"

"Yes. You see, the night before, I had gone out to the
terrace around midnight. I heard Tina open the
bedroom window above me. She said to someone that
the rain had stopped and it was time for the person to
go. It was Carlo. I saw him come down the stairs and
go out the door."

"So you knew—"

"Yes, that's when I knew they must have been lovers. Then, in the morning, when she was so excited, she told me Carlo had promised to see me and talk things over. She was sure he would agree to back off. I knew she was lying, but I had no idea what she had in mind.

"When Carlo came, we were on the terrace, and he asked me to go to the bottom of the garden. We each waited for the other to speak. Carlo was standing with his hands behind his back, evidently a habit of his, as she must have known. Then Tina cried out and ran down the steps toward me, telling me to watch out, that Carlo had a knife. She had a long kitchen knife in her hand and gave it to me, screaming, 'Kill him, kill him!'"

Andrew stopped, breathing deeply.

"You see, Jane, he was *not* holding a knife. After what Tina said, he pulled a knife from his back pocket and held it over me, but I simply looked at him and tossed away the knife I was holding. He punched me in the stomach, and I was knocked out for a minute or two. That's when he turned on Tina. You can imagine his fury. He knew she had betrayed him, and worst of all, he knew she wanted him dead."

Jane trembled. "She took an awful chance, Andrew. He might have killed you!"

"Remember, if I hadn't known she was lying, I would have struck at him, believing it was in self-defense, before he even got the knife out of his pocket. That would have tidied up everything for her. Carlo out of the way. All the money. And me. That is, until somebody else came along."

"Did you tell any of this to the Italian police?"

"No. My first instinct was to say nothing, and that hasn't changed. Carlo would simply deny having said what I heard, and there's no hard evidence against him. He'll certainly spend time in prison for Tina's murder, in any case."

"Is all this going to be a problem for you in doing the Marini biography?"

Andrew shook his head. "No, I don't think so. I'll certainly need to keep busy, and I'm glad Tina made the papers available to me, whatever her motive was. It does make me wonder how far back she planned the whole thing. She asked my department chair if I had a family, and learned that my wife had died. She had seen my picture on a book cover before she invited me to stay at Casa Marini. I think she decided even then that I would make the ideal witness for the disposal of her husband."

Jane said, "Now I have something to tell you that concerns Piero Marini's death, although it may never be made public."

"Yes?"

"When I went up to Keswick last week, I went to the house by the lake, hoping I could reconstruct what had happened. I thought Tina might have seen something without realizing its significance. But what I found was disturbing. First, she could not have heard the splash when her father fell in the lake, as she was in bed and her windows would have been closed against the cold. Then, as I sat in her window seat, I remembered what I heard at the party in Hampstead.

"A woman behind me was gossiping with Clifford Cox about Gerry Foster being there at the time Marini died and how dreadful for her, and Clifford said yes, it was, poor dear. Marini was even wearing an old polka-dotted macintosh of Gerry's when he was drowned, and it was thick with mud when they brought up the body. She could never look at it again. Here's the point. We knew about the mac from the transcript of the inquest. What we didn't know was that its pattern was in *polka dots!*

"Now, I realized the little girl was looking out the window at a hooded figure with its back to her, sitting on the bench at the end of the jetty, wearing Gerry Foster's mac, the polka dots recognizable in the dark. This was her chance to get rid of the hated rival to her father's affections. She runs softly down the back stairs in her slippers, and from the music room she hears the sound of the piano, where she assumes Marini is working on his sonata. She creeps out onto the jetty and gives a mighty push."

"But surely Gerry could swim?"

"Ah, yes, but she had fallen a few days before and her leg was in a cast! She would have sunk like a rock, or at least a child would presume that she would. Now Tina runs back up to her room and sees no sign of any disturbance in the water. Once she is sure it's too late to save Gerry, she runs down the stairs and pretends to look out in the garden and in all the rooms for her father. But why not look in the music room first?

"Then, when she does go to the music room, she sees, not her beloved Babbo, but Gerry standing there—and *that's when she screams!* Not when she supposedly thinks her father has fallen in the lake, but when she sees Gerry Foster!

"Now she knows it was Gerry she heard at the piano, not her father, and the horror of what she has done nearly destroys her. No wonder she had nightmares for years!"

Andrew's eyes were wet with tears. "Poor child! Poor Tina!"

Jane blinked back tears of her own. "Yes, it's been haunting me ever since that she had to live with this horror the rest of her life."

Andrew frowned. "I had thought all along that

Gerry Foster had something to do with Marini's death, although I couldn't put it together."

"I saw her again at the house, Andrew. She's a perfectly sensible and charming lady, with a special problem. Clifford Cox told me about her illness, and Gerry confirmed it herself. She has no recollection, of course, of our first encounter at the lake.

"You know, Andrew, I suppose we thought for a long time of the counterparts in the poem 'Christabel,' seeing Gerry as the sorceress Geraldine, and Tina as the innocent Christabel. Now I believe we had it reversed. At the party in Hampstead, I was looking at Tina when she saw Gerry Foster, and her eyes sort of shrank up with pure hatred—'venom' was the word that came to my mind. In the poem, serpent imagery is constantly associated with the evil woman. If Gerry was the intended victim, the innocent one—"

Andrew's voice thickened. "Yes. Then Tina was what Carlo called her. When she was dead and he was weeping, he kept saying *strega!* A witch, a sorceress. And he was right."

Later that afternoon, when Andrew had gone, Jane had a phone call from Susie Brecht, who had come to London to meet her friend Bill.

"Susie! Come on over—you can help me chase Laura around the flat!"

The two young women embraced, exclaiming over the tragedy of Tina's death.

Jane poured them each a drink. Susie sat down and held out her arms to Laura, who studied her for a moment and then consented to be lifted onto Susie's lap.

"Would you believe, it happened the day I left Florence?" Susie shook her head. "I heard it on the news here in London. 'Daughter of famous composer,' and all that. I knew Carlo was nuts about her, but I never imagined he'd go that far! Poor Andrew—how's he taking it?"

Having agreed with Andrew that, except for James, no one would ever hear the full story of Tina, Jane said, "He was just here. It's going to take time, but he'll be all right."

"Good. I went to see Emilia and Edmund yesterday. Just about what I would have expected. Emilia is having hysterics and carrying on as if she really cared, but poor Edmund is the one who's grief-stricken. He may be the world's leading phony, but he's a kindhearted phony, if you know what I mean, and he really loved Tina."

Jane gave Susie a compassionate look. "I expect you did too."

Susie frowned. "Look, Jane, you're an up-front sort of person. I'll tell you the truth. I was a good friend to Tina, more or less through thick and thin, but 'love' her? No. She was a selfish little beast, and an awful liar. She was probably playing Carlo and Andrew against each other, if I know Tina, and she got caught out. Men have been flipping over Tina all her life."

"You told me you were with Mario before he met Tina?"

"Right. It took me a while to get over that one, but Mario was a pretty violent guy. I was better off in the end without him."

Laura, who found this conversation less than absorbing, wriggled down from Susie's lap and addressed herself to her basket of toys, while Susie went on. "It looks as if Carlo nearly got Tina that night in Hampstead. Just helped himself to the knife in Edmund's cabinet and sneaked in the other door while Andrew thought he was standing guard."

"Yes. Susie, when we met in Florence, in the piazza, Edmund had that very knife in his pocket and looked really embarrassed when we saw it. Why was that, I wonder?"

Susie grinned. "I think he had paid a pretty penny for it—he has no sense with money—and didn't want to appear extravagant when he was there to beg money from Tina."

"Yes, it figures."

Jane said, "So what will happen with Carlo now?"

"He'll do some time, that's for sure. He'll have plenty of sympathy as the wronged lover, but that won't keep him out of prison."

"And how's Alex?"

"You won't believe this, Jane. You know how things never end at the right time for both people? Well, this time I think I lucked out. Alex has been showing signs of being ready to move on."

"Anyone special?"

"No, I think he's just cruising. But here's the great news. My old pal Bill is here from the States. Ever since his divorce, he's been sort of waiting in the wings for me, so to speak. I liked him a lot, but I think it put me off that my parents were so keen for him. He's a stockbroker, like my dad, and that *sounds* so stodgy."

"Did your parents ever meet Alex?"

"Oh lord, no. Mother would have flipped. The thing is, Jane, I've spent the last three days with Bill—the first time we ever really got together, if you know what I mean. And let me tell you, stodgy is not it. This guy is a dream. And I think I'm ready for some stability in my life, especially when Bill is part of the package!"

Three weeks later Andrew Quentin accepted an invitation from an old friend to spend the Christmas holidays with him in Rome, before going back to the States for the next term at the university.

His talk with Jane, and later with James as well, had eased some of the immediate pain of the tragic affair with Tina, but it would be a long time before he felt whole again. Most of the anger that had consumed him in the beginning had given way to overwhelming pity that a woman so beautiful, with so much to give, had had so little capacity for giving.

Going into the agency in London to book his ticket, he began to say "London to Rome" and found himself saying, "Put me into Pisa, then Rome to Los Angeles."

Until that moment, he had wanted to avoid going back to Florence. Now it seemed important to be there, to face the memories, perhaps to exorcise them.

At Pisa he took the train into the city, got into the taxi queue at the station, and directed the driver to the road leading across the river and up the winding road toward Casa Marini.

The gates to the house were closed, and he wouldn't have gone in, in any case. He had said his good-byes to Anna and Luigi. There was nothing to add. It was important only to see the house once more.

Then up the road and along the narrow streets where he had taken his daily walks, scarcely looking now at the view of the city below, shrouded in December mist.

Back down the main road toward the Piazzale Michelangelo. But first, the church of San Miniato.

Asking the driver to wait, Andrew climbed the long flights of stone steps and entered the interior of the church, his eyes drawn to the golden altar while they adjusted to the darkness. Then slowly he turned to his left and walked along the aisle to the little chapel with the madonna that had so fascinated him.

There she was, the blue robe draped over her knees, her gown a glowing red, the filmy veil covering her hair, and the exquisite face—Tina's face—almost but not quite smiling.

His heart twisting, he remembered Tina's sweetness. Like the lady Geraldine in the poem, she showed only gentleness and purity to the world, with no hint of the taint beneath the surface. Madonna or sorceress? Both.

Andrew turned and walked out of the church, back down the stone steps to the taxi, and rode in silence to the station to get his train to Rome.